To Live Again

by V. L. Edwards

First Edition

Copyright © 2015 by Vikki Vaught

Cover design by Dawné Dominique

All rights reserved. No part of this book may be reproduced in any form or by any electronic or mechanical means including information storage and retrieval systems, without permission in writing from the author. The only exception is by a reviewer, who may quote short excerpts in a review.

This book is a work of fiction. Names, characters, places, and incidents either are products of the author's imagination or are used fictitiously. Any resemblance to actual persons, living or dead, events, or locales is entirely coincidental.

ISBN:1517517087
ISBN-13:9781517517083

Dedication

This has been such an exciting journey for me and many friends helped me along the way. My thanks go out to all the members in my Smoky Mountains Romance Writers Chapter of RWA. Without their friendship and support, this book would not be what it is today. I want to thank Carolynn Carey in particular, who was kind enough to help me by reading my very raw manuscript. I would also like to thank Angelina Barbin, my critique partner, a fellow member of the Beau Monde Chapter of RWA. Her excellent feedback, regarding historical detail helped immensely. Lastly, I want to thank my beloved husband, for he truly has the patience of a saint.

Chapter 1

- Spring 1818 -

Once the play ended, Warren De Winter continued sitting quietly in a secluded corner of his private box. After several minutes passed he stood and glanced around the rapidly emptying theater. He was about to embark on the real purpose of his outing tonight, a purpose which didn't have anything to do with the play. He needed to exercise caution. He cringed at the thought of how *le bon ton* would gossip if they saw the Earl of Broadmoor climbing into a dilapidated hackney coach outside Covent Garden.

After exiting the theater, Warren glanced around, looking for anyone who might recognize him. Not seeing anyone he knew—*Thank God*—he hailed a hackney and climbed in, telling the driver to wait. He scooted forward on the sticky hackney seat and wrinkled his nose. The stench of unwashed humanity tended to linger in these old carriages, making him wish once again that he could bring his town coach on these monthly excursions. He shouldn't be here at all. Most noblemen kept mistresses to meet their physical needs. They didn't need to skulk outside Covent Garden hoping to rent a whore for the night. Of course, he wasn't like most noblemen.

Warren's pulse raced as he scanned the street looking for a young woman with long auburn hair. He saw buxom blondes and long legged brunettes, however no women with auburn hair. He sighed in disappointment, but just when he began to tell the driver to take him home, he spied a young, very petite woman turn the corner and head toward the carriage. Climbing from the hackney, his heart skipped a beat when he met the hazel-green gaze of this charming creature with a heart-shaped face and small, dainty nose.

She was conservatively dressed for a whore, wearing a three-quarter length deep gold pelisse, frayed at the edges, with a deep green gown peeking out at the bottom. While he was certainly no judge of women's clothing, even he could see her attire was several years out of fashion. From the way her eyes kept darting around, searching for something or someone, he felt sure she looked for a patron.

As the young woman moved to walk past him he stepped in front of her. "Good evening. Would you be interested in some company? I would love to spend time with you this evening."

The young woman looked over at him, after hesitating for several seconds, she stammered, "I-I would be interested, sir. I…must tell you I w-want ten pounds."

He never paid more than a couple of pounds with the other whores he hired. However, this young woman met his requirements. "All right, I have a room close by. Come, I shall take you there." Offering her his arm, he helped her into the carriage and told the driver to take them to the Duck Inn.

The woman remained quiet, unlike other whores he had chosen in the past, and she didn't try to entice him, which he found odd, to say the least. It made him wonder if she had done this for long. It was actually a pleasant change. He usually asked them to be quiet since their constant chatter grated on his ears. Come to think of it, this young woman was well-spoken for a whore, which intrigued him even more.

The hackney slowed down and pulled to a stop. Warren exited and assisted the young woman out. He almost asked her for her name, but he refrained. He always made it a practice to never ask that. When they entered the establishment, the innkeeper bowed to him. "Good evening, sir. Ever'thin' is as ye like it. As usual." He acknowledged the innkeeper's greeting and led the young woman upstairs. He had gone there earlier and got the key from the innkeeper, leaving instructions to have the chamber ready for his return.

After they entered the room, he locked the door. "Go behind the screen and remove your clothes. You will find hot water to bathe yourself with and a robe. When you have finished come back to me."

The young woman's hands shook as she reached up to untie her bonnet and remove it. She lowered it, twisting the brim with her hands. Her lip trembled and her eyes looked glassy with tears as she bowed her head and followed his directions. Taken aback by this show of tears and nerves, he wondered if he had made a mistake. She did look quite young. However, as she had come willingly, he dismissed his concern.

Once she disappeared from sight, he lit a few more candles. The lamp behind the screen illuminated the woman's shadow. While he watched her disrobe, fierce desire stirred in his loins. As he continued to watch, he reached down and rubbed his cock, which grew bigger by the minute. She had petite, high, pert tits, and he couldn't wait to feast on them. If he were a betting man he would wager she had small berry-colored nipples, as he always preferred.

When the woman finished undressing, she stood perfectly still as if frozen, so he called out, "Please, come here." He heard her take a deep shuddering breath, it gave him pause, making him again question his decision to engage her services. By this time he was greatly aroused, he pushed his hesitation away again.

Just when he thought she wasn't coming from behind the screen, she stepped out, moved a few feet, and stopped. His breath caught when he saw her. The sheer, pale blue silk robe showed her luscious curves to advantage. She was everything he desired, plump breasts with deep pink nipples, alabaster skin with a small patch of auburn pubic hair. Her tiny waist and gently flared hips drove desire straight to his already aching cock. Reminiscent of the statues of the Grecian goddesses he had seen when he visited the British Museum, definitely an alluring young woman's body. Her graceful figure fed the fire deep in his belly.

However, as he observed the pensive expression on her delicate face, he suspected she might be too fragile and young to handle such extreme sexual desires. "How old are you? Without your clothes, you look younger than I thought." As much as he would hate it, if she wasn't at least eighteen, he would need to send her on her way. While he enjoyed nubile young women, he refused to engage in sexual congress with a child.

"I j-just celebrated my twentieth b-birthday last week." Rushing her words, she added, "I'm old enough."

Thank God.

His desire reached fever pitch as he took in her womanly curves. It would have killed him to turn her away. "Ah, excellent. Slip the robe off so I can see the rest of you."

A blush rose up her cheeks, as she pulled the sash apart. The robe slipped from her shoulders and fell to the floor. Her beauty left him breathless. Never, in the last three years he had done this, had he picked up such an exquisite female—and she belonged to him for the entire night. He stepped closer. In a husky voice, he murmured, "I'm going to blindfold you. I promise I won't hurt you."

She looked up. Her face paled, and her eyes grew large as she backed away. "No, please don't. How can I trust you? I just met you tonight."

Warren raised an eyebrow. "Come now. You're a woman who has sold her favors before. You meet new men all the time. It can be quite titillating to be blindfolded. All your other senses will be more acute. I'm giving you more than you'll earn in the next month for one night. Don't act missish. It's not as though you're a virgin."

Slowly nodding she gave her consent, and he tied a large red silk handkerchief around her head, took her surprisingly soft hand and guided her to the bed. He gently pushed her down. Her hands reached for the covers. "No, you shan't need them. I want to see your gorgeous body." The young woman shivered; it couldn't be from the temperature of the room. He had made sure the innkeeper kept a nice warm fire ready whenever he used this chamber, and it felt comfortable.

For some reason this young woman seemed nervous. From the way she gripped the sheets with her fists, clearly, she had never been blindfolded before. He could imagine what her next reaction would be, but then he dismissed his concern again. After all, she was a whore. Surely she had received odd requests before. Warren retrieved two cravats from the chest and walked back over. He swiftly removed his clothes, leaving his shirt on. He never took that off. Taking one of her hands, he lifted her arm and tied her wrist to the bedpost.

She cried out, "What...w-what are you doing? You...you promised you wouldn't hurt me. Please don't do this. You're s-scaring me." She struggled against the binding as he lifted her other wrist and tied it to the other post. Her breathing grew shallow, and she started crying.

He didn't want her to fear him, so he tried to infuse restraint and reassurance into his tone. "I shall not hurt you. I never allow anyone to touch me. That's why I tied your hands. I promise it will bring you immeasurable pleasure. Now, please don't fight me." When she opened her mouth to scream, he kissed her, stifling the noise. "Shush," he growled against her lips. He never kissed whores, nevertheless he couldn't allow her to scream—that might bring the innkeeper running. These forays were his secret, and he wanted to keep it that way. The scandal would be appalling to say the least if word ever got out. He would never want his activities to become public knowledge. His mother would be crushed.

Deepening the kiss, his tongue swept into her open mouth, and he had never tasted anything sweeter. While he continued to kiss her deep, her mouth became pliant and soft beneath his. Warren stroked his hands across her breasts, and her nipples grew taut under his touch. Leaving her lips, he ran a hot trail of kisses down to one glorious peak and sucked her turgid nipple into his mouth.

Even though she still trembled, he smelled her arousal, mixed with the heady scent of jasmine, causing his own desire to escalate higher than before. When she moaned, he gently ran his hand down to the center of her moist heat, nudging her slender thighs apart. By this time, the girl writhed and twisted upon the bed, obviously enjoying the sensations coursing through her body.

Sensing she would no longer fight him, Warren rained kisses down her belly, licking her navel on his way to her honey pot. Spreading her slick pink folds, he gazed, awed by the most tantalizing cunt he had ever seen. "So beautiful." He leaned down and licked her quim, drinking her cunny juice as it dripped from her love canal, the finest ambrosia of the gods. Settling his shoulders between her thighs, he breathed in the clean, musky scent. Desire, stronger than he had felt in years raged through him, hot blood surged to the nerve endings of his cock. His tongue probed deeply inside her, as he slurped up her hot crème flowing from her body.

Her hips started gyrating, trying to get closer to his mouth as he nibbled his way up to her hooded clitoris. It swelled as he used tongue and teeth, sucking the little bud into his mouth. His finger slid into her tight sheath. He was right. She must be new to whoring. The girl let out a high keening sound, coming apart under his tender assault. Her love juices squirted out, drenching his tongue and dripping down his chin. He couldn't believe how much this delectable young woman came. Fire blazed a path through his veins. Rising up, he thrust into her body. But wait—something wasn't right. When he tore through what could only be a virgin's barrier, the girl cried out.

"What the hell! How can you be a virgin?" Deeply seated inside her tight passage, he remained still, not wanting to cause her any more pain. "Shush, I know that hurt. I promise it shan't hurt again." He probably should pull out, but his control had vanished, and it was too late anyway. The damage was done. Her channel clenched tightly around his thick shaft and he couldn't hold back.

Feeling her body relax, he started stroking in and out. She uttered a moan, though not from pain this time—from pleasure. He kept the pace slow and smooth, but then his tenacious hold broke. Like a piston he pounded her hard as waves of the most incredible sensations raced through him. He reached down and touched her clitoris, wanting to bring her to another climax. Just when he thought he would die from the intense pleasure, her cunt gave a spasm, pulsing around his painfully swollen shaft. Assured that she had reached fulfillment, hot semen gushed out of his cock filling her tight channel.

His arms too weak to hold him up any longer, Warren collapsed on top of her from a climax of such fierce intensity, it stole the breath from his body. Lowering his head, he nuzzled her neck. His heart hammered and his breaths came in great gasps as his brain assimilated what had occurred.

Once his breathing regulated, he said, "Please forgive me. I'm sorry I hurt you. If I had known you were a virgin, I wouldn't have touched you." Then in bewilderment, he asked, "Why did you come with me tonight? You knew I thought you were a whore. Explain why you did this, because for the life of me I can't imagine why."

Her tears soaked the handkerchief tied around her head. Warren rolled off her and tried to pull her into his arms, but with her wrists still tied to the bedposts, he couldn't. He reached up, untied her and pulled off the blindfold, then pulled her to him. She buried her head against the sweat dampened shirt on his chest and sobbed. He stroked her shoulders, trying to sooth her, but to no avail, she continued to wail out her grief and pain. After what seemed an age, she cried herself to sleep. Obviously, he would find no answers tonight.

God, he felt like the worst kind of pervert. His gut told him something wasn't right from the very beginning. Her quiet demeanor in the carriage should have alerted him that all wasn't as it appeared. He should have picked up on the fear in her eyes. However, he had allowed lust to overrule common sense. His prick had done the thinking, because it sure as hell hadn't been his brain.

Devil take it. What had he done? He had taken an innocent young woman's virginity. Why did she come with him? By God, when she woke up, he would make her tell him why she did this. By the manner of her speech, she might very well be a gentlewoman. If what he suspected was true, he would be honor bound to marry the damn girl.

What the damnation have I gotten myself into!

Chapter 2

Light filtered through the window when Amelia Harrington opened her eyes the next morning. The bed beneath her felt different from the one in her rooming house, much softer and more comfortable. An odd aroma filled the air, reminiscent of the bergamot cologne her father always wore, yet mixed with something else she couldn't quite put her finger on. She stretched and felt a twinge of discomfort in a mysterious place between her thighs. Rolling over, her hand brushed the empty space beside her. Where were her brother and sister? They always slept together now. As the last vestige of sleep lifted, everything came back to her. She sat up, her eyes darting around the room, looking for the man. Thank goodness, she was alone.

She slumped back against the pillows as icy prickles raced up her arms. Not only had she given away her most precious gift—her virginity—now it was for naught. That viper had sneaked from the room without paying her the ten pounds. Amelia rolled over, buried her head against the pillow and sobbed. How would they survive?

The landlady would evict them if she didn't find some money right away, and she would have to take her brother and sister to the workhouse. Despair filled her soul. Now she would need to do this all over again. In fact, she would surely have to do this every night in the foreseeable future, if she wanted to keep a roof over their heads and food in their bellies. Worry for Justin and Carrie's well-being was driving her mad. Their earlier life had been in the countryside with her father and stepmother, but now she, her brother and sister lived in a rooming house near Haymarket. How far they had fallen.

Amelia tried to find employment when they arrived in London, however no one would hire her without references. Desperation took over when their money ran out last week. That was why she had sold her body last night. Well, crying wasn't going to solve anything. She wasn't one to cry, but Lord, this situation was enough to make anyone want to. She needed to dress and go to her brother and sister. They must have been terrified last night when she didn't come home.

Pulling the blanket around her, she climbed out of bed and went around the screen. There was still water in the basin, though cold, and she began to bathe. When she wiped between her legs, the cloth came away with streaks of blood on it — her virgin's blood. No wonder she was sore. Tears gathered in her eyes. Dashing them away, she stiffened her spine. She had to put it behind her and move on.

After Amelia finished dressing, she looked around the room and spied a hairbrush lying on the chest. Her hair was an unruly mess. She ignored the pain as she ruthlessly brushed the curls until all the tangles were gone. Using the hairpins she found behind the screen, she pulled it back into a tight bun at the base of her neck. Once she was presentable, she turned around and noticed a wad of bank notes lying on the table under the window. Her eyes grew wide when she counted over fifty pounds. This would be enough to get them well away from London and back to the country where things were less expensive.

Perhaps that man wasn't such a cad after all. She was the one who deceived him. The shock had resonated in the man's voice last night when he discovered her virginity. He'd been gentle after he realized, and something happened to her body she had never experienced before and doubted she ever would again. What could only be desire, coiled in the pit of her stomach, and her nether regions ached when she remembered all he had done to her. Now that they wouldn't starve, she could look back on last night with a new perspective.

Tucking the money into the square bodice of her gown, she turned around and headed for the door. Before she took two steps, the door opened and the man stepped inside the room. Amelia blushed to the roots of her hair. Embarrassed over what occurred the night before, she glanced away. "I thought you w-were gone."

The man cleared his throat. "No, I went downstairs and ordered us breakfast. It should be here any minute. Please sit. We need to talk. Let me introduce myself. I'm Warren De Winter. I failed to ask you your name last night. I desire to remedy that."

Amelia's heart pounded and her palms grew damp. Oh, Lord, she took his money. What would he do to her when he noticed it missing? Luckily, he walked over to the dresser and when he turned his back to her, she reached inside her gown and pulled out the cash without him seeing and laid it back down on the table. The tension eased and she took a seat, taking a deep breath to calm her nerves. "Good morning, sir. My name is Amelia Harrington."

A knock echoed through the room, coming from the door and he called out, "Enter." A young serving girl came in carrying a heavy tray laden with several covered bowls and plates. She set the tray down on the table, and the gentleman handed her a coin. She curtsied and left the room. After he sat in the chair across from her, Mr. De Winter took off one of the covers and smelled. "Ah, fresh bread with butter. Let us break our fast." Taking the cover off another plate, he revealed coddled eggs and bacon. He filled a plate with a bit of everything, set it in front of her on the table and proceeded to serve himself, placing a mound of bacon and kippers, along with a generous serving of eggs on his dish.

"Thank you. I am hungry. Breakfast is much appreciated." The food smelled heavenly. Amelia placed a bite of egg in her mouth and the flavors of cheese and onion with a hint of basil burst forth. While nerve-wracking to eat in front of this man, her belly ached from starvation, since she hadn't eaten the day before, having given her food to her brother and sister. She continued to devour the meal. Once she ate her fill, she sat back in her chair and realized Mr. De Winter was watching her intently.

His golden eyes raked over her, and pleasure rushed through her belly. Her nipples drew up tight and poked the front of her dress. His eyes fell to her breasts, and she looked down when her cheeks flushed with warmth. How could she be reacting like this to a man she barely knew? She had never experienced feelings like this before, but he was so incredibly handsome with dark chocolate-brown hair and broad shoulders. Amelia couldn't help reacting to his male beauty. Remembering how he towered over her when he stood in front of her the night before, she surmised that he must be close to six feet tall.

After settling back against his chair, he folded his arms. "Miss Harrington, I need to ask you a few questions. When you offered to sell yourself to me so willingly last night, I assumed you were an experienced woman, and yet you were a virgin. Why did you accept my offer?"

Amelia straightened her napkin to give herself time to collect her thoughts. Believing honesty would suit her purpose best, since it might gain some sympathy, she decided to tell him part of the truth. "I need the money desperately. No one will give me employment since I have two young children for whom I am responsible. We ran out of food yesterday. My landlady gave me until tonight to come up with the rent, or she's turning us out onto the streets. If I could earn some money, we could leave London and go back to the country where things are cheaper."

"So, you're not from London. What happened to your family—and who are these children you're responsible for? They can't be yours, obviously."

Amelia twisted her hands as her heart pounded in her chest. This man unnerved her to a great degree, doing everything in his power to intimidate her. She would *not* cower in front of him—she was stronger than that. "I'm sorry, sir. It's really none of your concern. If you'll give me the ten pounds you owe me, I can be on my way." There was no way she would give this stranger any more information regarding her circumstances.

"I mean you no harm," he told her. "I feel bad about last night, and I want to make amends. In fact, if you'll tell me your story, I shall give you that roll of bank notes you did have hidden down your dress."

Oh, Lord, he saw me with his money. Now, he must think I am a thief. Perhaps, it would be all right to tell him my story. With all that money, I would be able to get the children to the country and keep them for a good long while.

She had avoided his gaze up to this point, but now she looked straight at him. "Do you promise you'll give me the money?"

"Yes. Here's twenty pounds to show you I speak the truth." Mr. De Winter picked up the money and pulled out a twenty pound note and laid it on the table in front of her.

Amelia grabbed the twenty before he could change his mind and tucked it back down her gown. "All right...I'll tell you. My father and stepmother died last year, in a carriage accident. Since then I've been responsible for Justin and Carrie, my brother and sister. My father worked for Lord Hollingsworth as a steward. When Papa died, he didn't leave much money. The cottage we lived in belonged to his lordship, so when he hired a new steward we had to leave. I don't have any other family."

He leaned forward in his chair. "Hmm, I know Lord Hollingsworth. I believe I met your father when I attended a house party at Hollingsworth's estate about five years ago. If I remember correctly your father was a younger son of an earl, wasn't he? Why couldn't you go to your uncle for help?"

Oh lord, how could he know this? Why did I use his lordship's name? That was incredibly stupid. What rotten luck — not only did he know Lord Hollingsworth, he had actually met my father and knows I am related to the Earl of Sotheby.

"My father was estranged from his brother. I wrote to my uncle when he died, but he refused to help us."

"Where are your brother and sister right now? They must be quite worried that you didn't return last night. How old are the children anyway?"

Amelia looked over at him with tears in her eyes. Refusing to let them fall, she brushed them away, determined to be strong. "Justin is six and Carrie's a year older. That's why I need to leave straightaway. I'm sure they're terrified."

Mr. De Winter stood. "Come, I shall take you to them now. We can talk more in the carriage ride over there. I will give you the rest of the money when we arrive at your home. Now, where are your rooms?"

"Near Haymarket. I hate to be a bother. However, I will gladly accept a ride. I need to return to them as quickly as possible."

He led her outside to a hackney coach, and then they were off. As it turned out, the Duck Inn was close by, so they didn't have much time to talk. When they arrived at the rooming house, the landlady met her at the door, and she didn't look happy.

"Where the 'ell 'ave ye been, ye slut!" the woman screamed. "Ye left them two little brats all by themselves while ye were out whorin' around. I runs a decent 'ouse 'ere. Ye need to get yer stuff and get out of 'ere. I don't want no whore living in *my* 'ouse."

Mr. De Winter stared the old woman down. "You will not address my betrothed in that manner. Don't worry, madam. We are here to retrieve her belongings and the children. After that, we will be on our way. Now, let Miss Harrington pass while I settle her account, then we shall leave your abode in a matter of minutes."

Speechless, Amelia wasn't sure she had heard him correctly. Did he just refer to her as his betrothed? What could he be thinking?

Mrs. Cowell stepped aside when she heard the authority in his voice. Deciding he just wanted to protect her reputation, Amelia didn't contradict him, since that would not accomplish anything. She needed to pack their belongings and see the children. She hoped Mr. De Winter would give her the rest of that money and a ride to the coaching inn, so they could leave London for good.

Amelia flew upstairs. When she opened the door, Justin and Carrie ran to her and flung themselves against her. "Darlings, I'm sorry. I know you've been worried sick about me. Children, I have some wonderful news. We're going back to the country."

"Are we going back to our old house?" Carrie asked. "I hope so because I don't like it here anymore. Mrs. Cowell hit Justin last night when he started crying. She's mean."

Justin pulled on her skirt to capture her attention. "Why did you leave us last night? Mrs. Cowell hit me hard."

"I'm terribly sorry. I promise I will never leave you again. Now, help me pack so we can leave this place for good." After Amelia gave them a hug, she went to the chest, pulled out a valise and began stuffing their clothes inside it. Within fifteen minutes, all their belongings were packed. As she closed the last valise, someone knocked on the door, and she called out, "Who is it?"

"It's me, Miss Harrington." She heard Mr. De Winter's voice through the door. "I thought you might want some help carrying your things downstairs. I have a hackney coach waiting for us."

She rushed to the door and opened it. "Thank you, Mr. De Winter. How kind of you. Let me introduce you to my brother and sister." Putting her arms around their shoulders, she faced him. "This is Justin and Carrie."

"Good morning, it's a pleasure to meet you." Picking up two of the valises, he beckoned to them. "If you will follow me, we shall leave this horrid place forever. I settled everything with your landlady. You shan't have any more worries from her."

While taken aback by this, it relieved her mind that she wouldn't need to deal with Mrs. Cowell again. She only owed her three shillings. Knowing her, she told him a lot more. "Thank you, sir. I appreciate you giving us a ride. I hate to cause you this much trouble."

"Don't worry, it's my pleasure. Come, let us depart." He led them back downstairs and out to the carriage. Once they were all inside, the carriage pulled away. "It shouldn't take more than fifteen minutes to reach my townhouse. Once the children are settled, we will talk. For now, make yourself comfortable. It's been a hectic morning, and I'm sure you're tired."

Startled, Amelia glanced over at him, with some alarm. "Oh, we can't go to your townhouse. If you will be kind enough to give me the money, less whatever you paid my landlady, you can drop us off at the Golden Crown on the Great North Road, near St. Martin's Le-Grand, and we can be on our way."

"I promise it will be proper. I sent a note round to my aunt, and she will be waiting for us when we arrive at my townhouse. She will make sure the children are taken care of and have a maid watch them so we can talk. Now, don't worry about a thing, sit back and rest."

At this point Amelia accepted that she wouldn't accomplish anything if she continued this discussion. Once the children were put to rights, they were going to have a much needed conversation. He would give her the money and take them to the coaching inn or her name wasn't Amelia Harrington.

When they arrived at Mr. De Winter's townhouse, a footman came down the steps and assisted them out of the carriage. A tall, slender woman of middle years met them at the door.

Mr. De Winter gave the woman a warm smile, and then turned toward Amelia. "Miss Harrington, this is my aunt, Lady Willhoite, my late father's sister. She will show you and the children to the nursery, where they can play while we talk." Then addressing his aunt, he added, "Aunt Bernice, this is Miss Harrington and her brother and sister, Justin and Carrie. Thank you for coming quickly."

"No problem at all, uh…De Winter," Turning to Amelia, Lady Willhoite gave her a welcoming smile. "Charmed to meet you. If you will follow me upstairs, we shall settle the children. After that, you can come back downstairs to talk to…De Winter. No need to worry regarding the children, there are plenty of toys and such to keep them entertained."

Amelia wondered why Lady Willhoite paused every time she mentioned her nephew's name. Of course, what did it matter as long as she spoke to him, and received the money, so she dismissed it from her mind.

"It's a pleasure meeting you, Lady Willhoite. I appreciate your help." Amelia felt pushed by both Mr. De Winter and his aunt. She wanted to resist, but until she could meet privately with him, she needed to exhibit patience. Once they were alone, she would let him know what she thought of his strong tactics.

Lady Willhoite led her and the children upstairs, and they entered a well-appointed nursery. The children ran over to the shelves, crammed with all manner of interesting toys and dozens of books. Carrie found one filled with pictures and immediately started looking at it. Justin found some tin soldiers, and he soon had them lined up in battle formation. With all these play things to entertain them, it relieved her mind greatly to know that the children would be fine while she talked to Mr. De Winter.

"Can you find your way back downstairs?" Lady Willhoite asked.

"Yes, I'll be fine. I should be back shortly to gather the children so we can be on our way." Smiling over at Justin and Carrie, she told them, "I'm going downstairs to talk to the gentleman who brought us here. Please obey the maid and Lady Willhoite. Once I finish talking with him, we will leave for the country."

Carrie smiled up at her. "We will behave, I promise. I wish we could stay here. Look at all these wonderful books. I would love to look at all of them. It's been such a long time since I've looked at a book I can't remember all my letters."

Pain shot through Amelia's heart. She had tried so hard to survive she hadn't continued the children's education. Once they were settled, she would find some way to fix that. She didn't want Justin and Carrie growing up illiterate. "Children, enjoy your time here. I shall return soon."

It wasn't difficult to find her way back downstairs. The butler waited for her at the foot of the stairs and showed her to Mr. De Winter's study. When she entered the room, he stood and bowed to her.

"Please be seated. I trust the children are all settled? My aunt will make sure they are entertained."

Amelia stiffened her spine. "There is absolutely no reason for you to bring us to your townhouse. You should have given me the money and dropped me off at the coaching inn. I could be well on my way by now. With this delay, I will probably need to spend the night before I can find a mail coach going north. I don't appreciate your high-handedness." She took a deep breath, trying to calm herself. Great bursts of anger rushed through her to the point of needing to fight back tears. She refused to allow this man to see her vulnerability.

"How long do you think fifty pounds would last? I couldn't live with my conscience if I let you go off with those two young children. I took your innocence last night. You're a genteelly-raised young woman. Dammit! Your uncle is an earl, for God's sake. Even if you did accept my offer last night, the fact still remains, I ruined you. We shall be married once I procure a special license. My aunt has agreed to stay here until we can be married tomorrow."

Stunned, Amelia dropped down onto the chair and stared at him.

"Married? You want to marry me? I…I don't know what to say. I…never expected this." Lord, this might be the answer to all their problems, yet—to enter a marriage of convenience? She had always hoped to meet someone and fall in love. As attractive as she found this man, she certainly didn't love him, and in no way did he love her, but did she have any choice? She had to do what was best for the children. Oh lord, should she take advantage of him? Though, there again, she wasn't forcing him to marry her.

Mr. De Winter came around his desk and took her hand in his and met her eyes with a deep penetrating look. "I know we met under unusual circumstances. Nonetheless, I will be a good husband, and I'll help you raise your brother and sister. You will never want for anything. I'm a wealthy man, and I can provide Justin with an excellent education. I have a son the same age, and I'm sure they will become good friends. Carrie will have a dowry when it comes time for her to marry."

The trepidation that gripped her, eased a bit. If he had a son, then perhaps, he would be a good father figure for her brother and sister. "You have a son?"

He hesitated. "Yes, my wife died three years ago. I promise to give your siblings the same care and understanding I give to my son. I'm sure with time, we will rub along nicely, and I'm certainly attracted to you. Please say you will accept my hand in marriage."

This is too good to pass up.
The children would be set for life, and I do find him attractive.
Yes, I will do it.

Amelia looked down at the strong hand holding hers. "If you're sure, then yes...I'll marry you. I promise I will be a faithful wife. Thank you. With time, I'm sure you're right, we will get along well." A shiver of apprehension raced through her when she remembered him blindfolding her and tying her up the night before. Though for whatever reason, she wasn't afraid of him. He must have a logical reason for his behavior, and she was immensely drawn to him. "I-I'm attracted to you, too."

"You shall not regret marrying me, I promise. I will ring for my housekeeper, Mrs. Goodall, and she will escort you to your room. Oh, by the way, we should start calling each other by our given names, don't you think? Amelia?"

"All right...Warren." He pulled her up and kissed her, plunging his tongue deeply into her mouth. Desire burned throughout her entire body. Thrills of delight shot to her womb when her body remembered what it had experienced the night before. No, the marriage bed wouldn't be something they would have a problem with, other than they might burn each other up. She might be an innocent, or at least she had been before last night, but this passion they felt for each other had to be rare. All thought fled from her mind as he swept her into a vortex of pleasure.

Just as Warren raised her skirt, someone knocked on the door. He reluctantly let her go. "Who is it?"

Through the door, a female voice called out, "It's Mrs. Goodall, sir."

"Ah, yes, come in." A plump, yet pleasant looking woman of middle years entered the room. Amelia took to her immediately, and that was a good thing, since she would soon be running this household.

Her betrothed moved to her side, raised her hand to his lips, and kissed it as he looked at the housekeeper. "Good morning, Mrs. Goodall. This is Miss Harrington, my betrothed. Please show her to the blue room. I believe you keep it ready for unexpected guests."

"Congratulations, sir. I would be happy to escort her." Mrs. Goodall curtsied to Amelia. "It's a pleasure to meet you, Miss Harrington. If you will follow me, I'll take you to your room."

Warren looked over at her. "Miss Harrington, I shall see you at dinner."

Amelia met his gaze and saw the remnants of passion lingering in the golden depths. A sharp stab of desire shot straight to her feminine core as she said in an unsteady voice, "Until this evening, Mr. De Winter." Then she followed the housekeeper from the room.

Oh, why did the housekeeper have to interrupt them at that moment? Her body ached for fulfillment. A burn, deep within her belly had her wanting to scream her frustration. However, if the woman had caught them in the act, she would have died of mortification. Thank goodness, she had knocked before Warren took her clothes off. It would have been truly embarrassing, to say the least.

No – I shan't have a problem with the marriage bed.

Chapter 3

After Mrs. Goodall led Amelia upstairs, Warren sat back down at his desk. He was getting married again. Something he had never expected, nor wanted. He couldn't have lived with his conscience if he just gave her some money and sent her on her way. Besides, he had never felt such lust for someone before. Look at how close he came to ravishing her in his study a few moments before. If Mrs. Goodall hadn't shown up when she did, he would have had the chit naked and pumping his cock deep inside her delectable cunt. In fact, he needed some release. His prick throbbed from their brief encounter. There was something about this young woman that caused a fire to burn deep inside him.

He went over and locked the door, then sat down and pulled his stiff erection out of his breeches. While stroking his aching shaft, he pictured her lying on the desk naked with all that glorious auburn hair cascading down around her shoulders and breasts. He would spread her honey pot open wide and lap up her crème pouring from her tight little passage. While he fantasized, he pumped his cock faster and faster, imagining being deep inside her. He would fuck her so hard and long he'd have her screaming her release. He had never experienced a woman as responsive as Amelia.

His balls drew up snug against the base of his cock. Ready to explode, he grabbed a handkerchief and caught the streams of semen ejaculating out of the end of his shaft. Something else he liked concerning her — she could handle all of him, and some women couldn't. In some ways it was a curse, having such a large instrument of pleasure. The last waves of release rolled through him, and he slumped back against the chair. With his eyes closed, he imagined her cleaning up all his semen, licking his prick clean and smiling up at him. Ah, yes, he would enjoy teaching her all the wicked ways they could enjoy each other's bodies.

As pleasant as all this daydreaming had been, he needed to get to Doctors' Commons. He needed to purchase that special license for tomorrow. Oh yes, marriage to Amelia wouldn't be a hardship. He may have met his sexual match.

Warren spent all afternoon getting the special license, and it cost him quite a few coins to accomplish it. He worried over the decision to not tell her of his title. She thought he was a plain mister. She was already worried over marrying him, and he didn't want to add to her concerns regarding their upcoming nuptials. Once they married, he would broach the topic after she was so sexually sated she'd be willing to accept him even if he were the King of England.

After Warren left the commons with the special license in his pocket, he climbed into his carriage and made his way over to

Boodles to find his friend, Mallory, Viscount Rutherford. They had been friends since Eton, and he looked forward to seeing the shocked look on Mallory's face when he found out he was getting married again. His friend, a confirmed bachelor and rake, vowed to never marry. He tried to encourage Warren to join in on some of his sexual escapades over the last three years, but he always refused.

Mallory didn't know of his monthly search for a whore. He believed Warren had remained celibate since Lucinda died. He would never tell Mallory how he and Amelia met. That was a secret he would take to his grave. She would be ostracized if anyone ever found out she sold herself for ten pounds. Her actions proved how desperate she was. What he did understand about Amelia, she would do whatever it took to take care of Justin and Carrie. She wouldn't need to worry any longer. It was now his responsibility to protect her and the children.

Once Warren arrived at Boodles, he entered the card room and spied Mallory seated at a table engaged in a game with another one of their friends. Stallings stood when he walked over.

"Good afternoon, gentlemen. Care if I join you?"

Stallings grinned. "You can take my place, Broadmoor. I'm leaving. My wife and I are going to a ball in Richmond tonight. If I don't return home soon she will have my head on a platter. Good to see you again. Gentlemen, I bid you farewell."

He took the seat Stallings had vacated. "Mallory, I'm glad I found you. I have some news. I'm getting married tomorrow…"

"What did you say?" Mallory leaned forward in the chair, bracing his hands on the table. "Who the hell are you marrying?

I thought you vowed to never marry again. You swore to mourn Lucinda for the rest of your life. Damn, you've lived the life of a hermit for three years. When have you had an opportunity to meet someone?"

Warren ran a finger around the neck of his cravat, trying to loosen the stranglehold it had on him. He needed to handle this carefully, or Mallory would see right through his story. "Her name is Amelia Harrington. I met her years ago when her father was the steward for Lord Hollingsworth. You remember Oswald Harrington. We both met him at that house party we attended back in 1813. Through the years I kept in touch with him. He gave me some good advice which helped my crop yields dramatically."

"But what the hell does that have to do with you marrying his daughter," Mallory interrupted. "How old is this chit anyway?"

Warren kept his tone even as he answered, "Miss Harrington's twenty, but why does that matter? If you'll let me finish, I'll explain."

"By all means," he retorted, "tell me the rest."

He took a deep calming breath. "When Harrington and his wife died last year in a carriage accident, his children were left with very little blunt. Amelia's uncle, the Earl of Sotheby, refused to help her. Once Lord Hollingsworth found a new steward, she had to move. She and her two young siblings came to London several months ago. It hasn't been easy for her. Finally, she came to me and asked for my help."

Mallory raised his eyebrows. "Help is one thing, marriage is another. I still don't understand why you're marrying the chit."

Meeting his friend's gaze, he leaned in. "You know my mother wants me to remarry. Lawrence needs a mother, and when I saw how well she takes care of her brother and sister, I realized she would make an excellent one."

"Hmm, so you're marrying her for your son. What does she look like?" he drawled. "I can't see you marrying an ugly one, not after marriage to such a beautiful woman as Lucinda. Couldn't you hire her as a governess for Lawrence? If she's struggling financially, she would probably jump at permanent employment."

"Governesses can leave, and they don't allow themselves to love their charges. As far as her appearance, Amelia's lovely. I'm quite attracted to her. While I shall never give my heart again, I have decided I wouldn't mind having a woman to warm my bed. There's nothing more to it." Warren watched Mallory's face. If he accepted his story, then everyone else would be easy.

His friend threw his head back and laughed out loud. "So, you've at last gotten tired of your lonely existence. It's about time, my friend. I would rather have seen you take a mistress. Of course, I have always known you were too upstanding for my rakish ways. What a shame, because we could have had some riotous good times. Are you sure you won't change your mind? I have plans tonight with two soiled doves from Lavern's Pleasure Palace. We could have made it a foursome instead of a ménage a trois. I never mind sharing and besides, I love watching."

Warren rolled his eyes. "My friend, you'll never change. You know I would never let anyone watch me. I'm a very private person. The sight of my scars would turn your stomach, and no woman would ever want to touch me."

Mallory grew serious. "I'm sorry. I forgot how self-conscious you are. But, what are you going to do? Have sex with your clothes on all the time? Surely, you'll allow your wife to see you. Can the scars be that bad?"

"I'm grotesque," he muttered, "but I'll manage somehow. The dark hides a multitude of sins." Warren could see the pity in Mallory's eyes and it cut him deep. He hated anyone's pity. At least he believed Mallory accepted his story and thought he was marrying Amelia for Lawrence's sake and to have a woman in his bed. "What I really came to ask — will you stand with me tomorrow? It would mean a great deal to me."

"Of course, my friend. I would be honored. Tell me where and when, and I shall be there."

"The ceremony will be at St. Paul's Cathedral tomorrow at eleven o'clock." Warren stood. "Since I have quite a few things to take care of, I'll be on my way. Thank you again for standing up with me. I shall see you tomorrow." He shook Mallory's hand and left the club.

Once he returned to his carriage, he told the driver to take him to Garrard's so he could pick out a ring for Amelia. While there were plenty of rings in the family vault, he wanted to give her something which would be all her own, not some hand-me-down from a past countess.

After he arrived at Garrard's, Warren found a gorgeous oval emerald with diamonds circling it. When he saw it, he wanted the ring for her. It would bring out the green in her amazing hazel eyes. He also bought her a pair of emerald earbobs. He imagined nibbling on her delectable earlobe with those emeralds in her ears. His cock stood at attention, just thinking about it. In fact, every time he thought of her, he ended up in the same condition.

After his conversation with Mallory, he did worry about keeping all the scars from her. He couldn't tie her up every time he wanted to have sexual congress with her, and he planned on having sex often. None of the whores he had hired over the last three years caused the raging inferno of desire in him that Amelia did.

With Lucinda, it had been all so proper. She had never seen him without his nightshirt and back then he'd had nothing to hide. He had gone to her, gently raised her night rail and entered her as chastely as possible. What he felt for Lucinda was totally different because he had *loved* her. With all the others since her death, it was about feeding his sexual appetite.

With this young woman, he could let himself go in a way he had never been able to do before. Love wouldn't play a part in their relationship because his heart would always belong to Lucinda. It was different with Amelia. He could let his lust go with complete abandon, not holding back in any way with her. No doubts entered his mind—she could handle it. That siren had as much fiery passion in her as he had.

When Warren arrived back at his townhouse he spoke with the butler, Abercrombie, regarding the arrangements for the wedding breakfast the next day. He also met with Mrs. Goodall, finalizing all the details.

His aunt waylaid him on his way upstairs. "Broadmoor, did you purchase the special license?"

He smiled down at his aunt. "Yes, all is arranged. The vicar at St. Paul's agreed to marry us tomorrow at eleven. I finalized everything for the wedding breakfast, and Lord Rutherford agreed to stand with me, so everything is set. How is Miss Harrington?"

"I think she is taking everything in her stride. Oh, Broadmoor, I like her a great deal and the children are captivating. Lawrence will be thrilled to have some children to play with. She didn't have anything to wear tomorrow, so I sent for my dressmaker. She brought over a lovely gown for her. I don't know the story of how you met and it is none of my business, however, I do feel you've made a wise decision. I know you never planned to marry again, but she will be a loving mother for your son."

Knowing he needed to tell her something, he told his aunt the same story he told his friend. Thank God, she accepted it without question.

"Aunt, I'm going upstairs so we'll talk more over dinner. Oh by the way, I have sent word to my mother, and she and Clayton should be able to attend. I asked her to bring Lawrence with them. That way he can meet Amelia and the children."

"I'm glad they will be able to come. I'm sure Sophie is ecstatic over you getting married again, and I know she is going to love Amelia. I shall take my leave now. I will see you at dinner."

That evening, Amelia was quiet while eating their evening meal. Warren realized she wasn't much of a talker. It didn't bother him because most females he knew talked too much. Aunt Bernice eventually brought her out of her shell. While he watched her talking with his aunt regarding the upcoming wedding, the candlelight from the candelabra cast a glow which illuminated her creamy skin—her beauty mesmerized him. He might not have planned on marrying, but at least he took comfort knowing his betrothed was such a beautiful young woman.

After dinner ended, he followed the ladies to the drawing room instead of drinking port in his study. At ten o'clock, Aunt Bernice excused herself and retired for the night.

Warren took a seat beside her on the blue dupioni silk settee. "My dear, you're terribly quiet this evening. Are you all right?"

Amelia looked over at him and tears shone in her eyes. "I feel terrible about trapping you into this marriage. If I were a stronger woman, I would have turned you down, but I have to consider what is best for the children. I really didn't have anywhere to go and no money. It's so unfair that you must bear the consequences of my reckless actions."

He put an arm around her slender shoulders. "I'm adjusted to the thought of this marriage. My mother has wanted me to remarry for two years, so I could find someone to be a mother for my son. After watching you with your brother and sister today, I know you'll be a good one. Since Lawrence was three when my wife died, he doesn't remember her."

She gazed at him. "How did your wife die?"

He sighed. As hard as it was to talk about Lucinda, Amelia needed to know he would never be able to love her. He hoped he would be able to explain without hurting her feelings.

"I lost my wife when my home caught fire. My son's nurse got him downstairs, and I removed them from the house. I went back for my wife, and as I ran up the stairs, a ceiling beam fell on me. My servants barely got me out before the whole staircase collapsed."

"Oh my, how horrible!" she gasped. "You could have been killed, but thank goodness, you survived."

After he took a deep breath, Warren continued with his story. "Just barely. I nearly lost my life. It took me months of recovery before I was up and about again. If it weren't for my son, I would have given up when they told me my wife perished in the fire. Lucinda was my life, my heart and my soul.

I don't want to hurt you, but you need to understand I can't give you my love. I buried my heart with Lucinda."

Amelia reached over and touched his hand. "I'm sorry you suffered all that. I can imagine how painful it was losing your wife. While I've never known romantic love, I did love my father and stepmother tremendously and when they died, the children were what kept me sane. I had to remain strong so I could protect them."

"That's what I do know about you. You'll do anything for those children. You willingly sold your virginity to feed them." He lifted her chin and looked at her. "What I can promise you, is a faithful husband. While I can never love you, I do desire you greatly, and I think you return my desire. That's more than many marriages of the *ton* have."

With a gentle touch, he pulled her close and tenderly kissed her mouth, but as soon as his lips met hers, a flame burst in his belly and he ravished her mouth.

Amelia feverishly returned his kiss. Passion swept him away as he slipped a hand inside the bodice of her gown. Her nipple furled up into a tight berry. "Damn, you have the nicest breasts." Tugging down the front of her gown, he leaned down and sucked her turgid nipple into his mouth while he rolled the other one between his thumb and forefinger.

She moaned as she ran her fingers through his hair. He pulled up the hem of her gown and slid his hand up her slender thighs to the patch of auburn hair covering her honey pot. Slipping his fingers down her clitoris, he felt her moist heat. Unable to resist, he fell to his knees, opened her thighs wide and leaned in, delighting in the wild scent of her quim. While stroking her love bud with his tongue, he pushed two fingers into her sheath and started working her. The more he stroked, the wetter she became. Crème dripped from her and he lapped it up like a cat licking milk.

"You have the best tasting honey pot. I could eat you all night." Fire rushed through his loins, pervading all the nerve endings in his body. He needed to feel her tight cunt around his cock. "I can't wait any longer, I've got to fuck you." Ripping down his breeches and smalls, he pushed deep inside her. Wild bursts of pleasure raced through his body as he used firm vigorous strokes, ever pushing higher and higher to that pinnacle of desire.

He wanted to feel Amelia clench his shaft when she reached her peak. He reached down and lightly squeezed her love bud, and she went spinning off into the void. Her tight passage clamped around him as he pumped ever faster. Then he exploded and his essence filled her. He tenderly kissed her lips and hugged her close. Gasping breaths of air, he choked out, "I can't seem to leave you alone. You've started a fire in me, my dear."

"I feel the same way," she whispered. "I never realized how much I would enjoy this. Anytime you want to, what did you call this? I think you called it…fuck. Umm, I'm ready to…uh, fuck whenever you want. Perhaps we should do it in a bedchamber next time. If one of the servants walked in on us, I would be mortified."

"I promise we'll use the bedchamber, once we are married. Now, let me escort you upstairs. You shall need a great deal of rest for the day to come." His body tensed at the thought of their wedding night. He had just fucked her moments ago, and he already wanted her again!

"You're going to need plenty of sleep, because I don't think you'll get much tomorrow evening. I shall keep you busy throughout the night." Pushing up off the settee, he stood and buttoned his fall. He offered her his hand and helped her up. "After all, tomorrow is our wedding day."

Of course, he did need to figure out how to keep her from seeing his scars. Although he would hate it, he would keep a night shirt on, but damn he wanted to be skin to skin with her. He needed to give some serious thought to all this. Thank God, she was such an innocent. Perhaps she wouldn't understand why he tied her up. Mayhap, she would accept it as part of his lovemaking. He would have to make her so hot and filled with desire, she would forget what he was doing to her.

Ah, yes, that plan just might work.

Chapter 4

Warren gave her a chaste kiss on her cheek when he left her at her bedchamber door. In a daze, Amelia entered the beautifully appointed room she hadn't given a glance earlier that day. She looked around the spacious area, taking in the furnishings and the paintings hung on the soft pale blue walls. A small gilded writing desk sat between the velvet draped windows, and the curtains and counterpane adorning the bed were a deeper blue, matching the drapes. Now she understood why he called it the blue room. She still didn't have the wherewithal to appreciate the elegance and beauty.

The magnitude of what she had agreed to blasted through her like a winter snow storm. Oh dear, was she making the right decision? Everything had happened so quickly, it had her reeling. Tomorrow she would marry a man she only met twenty-four hours ago. Of course, only a foolish young woman would let this opportunity pass her by. What he offered her meant the difference between her and the children living with every luxury Warren could provide or living in abject poverty.

At least intense passion blazed between them, which was more than many marriages started off with. Perhaps love could come later. First they needed to take the time to get to know each other. Warren was obviously an honorable man, or he would never have insisted on them getting married. Her instincts told her she could trust him. She had been the deceitful one since they met. Her behavior, her choices led them to this point, not his. Some men could grow resentful. She prayed her instincts were correct, and he wouldn't hold this marriage against her later.

A knock sounded on the bedchamber door.

"Who is it?" she called out.

A young girl's voice answered. "Me name is Susan, Miss Harrington, th' upstairs maid. I'm here t' help ye get ready fer bed."

Goodness, her future position was going to take some getting used to. No one had helped her undress, since she was a small child.

"Please come in."

The maid entered the room and curtsied. "I've ordered ye a bath, miss. The water should be here any minute."

"Thank you, Susan. A warm bath will be lovely." Another knock at the door interrupted their conversation. Two footmen carried in large pails of steaming water. Soon, a brass tub in a small room she hadn't noticed earlier was filled with the hot water. Great whirls of steam rose above the surface. The scent of jasmine permeated the air, and Amelia couldn't wait to submerge herself in all those bubbles. Over the last six months, she'd made do with sponge baths. There was no privacy at Mrs. Cowell's house, just a communal bathing room off the kitchen.

Once the footmen left, Susan helped her prepare for her bath. It embarrassed her when the young girl helped her disrobe. Now that she was marrying someone with money, she would need to get used to having a maid. Once Susan left her alone, she pondered the source of Warren's wealth. If his aunt had 'Lady' before her name, then he must be a gentleman. She doubted he was middle-class or a merchant. Her betrothed was probably a younger son of a lord, at the very least. Oh, Lord, what was she getting herself into? Would she be expected to attend balls and soirees?

A thrill of anticipation shot through her. The thought of being at a ball dressed in a gorgeous gown, sent shivers down her spine. As a young child, she had watched from afar while Lord Hollingsworth entertained lords and ladies, and she had imagined herself all grown up and part of the *ton*. While her father had been the son of an earl, an estrangement developed between her father and his family. She was never given the chance to move about in polite society.

How this marriage would change her family's lives seeped into her mind. Justin and Carrie would have all the advantages of being raised in an affluent household. Justin would receive the best education, be able to attend Eton or Harrow and mingle with the sons of the aristocracy. She would make sure Carrie had the best governess, so she could satisfy her thirst for learning. She had been terribly afraid her brother and sister wouldn't have a proper upbringing, and now she wouldn't need to worry about that anymore.

By this time, the water had cooled, so she finished her bath. When she entered her bedchamber, she found a delicate lawn night rail lying at the foot of her bed. Sure the maid would return any minute she quickly pulled it on over her head. She luxuriated in the feel of the fine fabric caressing her body. Going over to the overstuffed chair by the fire, she sat and ran the brush through her hair so it could dry.

With a tap on the door, Susan entered. "Miss, please let me help ye with yer hair. Take a seat in front o' th' mirror."

Still uncomfortable having a maid tend to her, Amelia sighed, then sat at the dressing table and allowed the young girl to brush her hair. It actually felt nice, and she found herself growing drowsy.

"That's enough, Susan. Please braid my hair, so it won't tangle while I sleep. I appreciate your help. I'm quite tired and ready for bed. You may go as soon as the braiding is done."

"As ye wish, miss. Ye got pretty hair, by th' way. It's a pleasure t' help ye with it. There, all braided and ready fer bed."

"Thank you, Susan. Goodnight."

Once the maid departed, she crawled in bed, but grew worried about the children. They weren't used to sleeping alone. Getting up, she pulled on an amber silk dressing gown the maid had left lying at the foot of the bed and headed for the nursery. She found them huddled together in one of the beds, crying. "Oh, my loves, please don't cry."

Carrie spoke up, her little lip quivering. "We missed you, sister. We don't like sleeping alone. The nursemaid who helped us dress for bed told us we couldn't sleep together, that it wasn't proper. I don't want to be proper if it means I can't be with you."

"Me neither," Justin chimed in. "I want to sleep with you, like we usually do. That girl told us you didn't have time for us. I knew she was wrong. You would *never* be too busy for me and Carrie."

Amelia sat on the bed and pulled them close. "No, darling, you're right. You must be speaking of Mary, the maid who took care of you when I came to see you before dinner. I will talk with her tomorrow. Now, I know it's difficult to understand, but we can't sleep together anymore. There's no need now that we have our own beds. Why don't I tell you a story, and then I shall tuck you in."

Amelia told them their favorite tale of King Arthur and his famous knights. Justin fell asleep before she finished the story. After tucking him in, she led Carrie back to her bed and settled her as well. By the time she turned down the lamp, her sister had fallen asleep.

After she entered her room, she slipped back into bed, so exhausted she felt sure she would fall asleep right away. But her mind wouldn't settle. She worried over all the changes happening to her and the children. While good changes, they were still overwhelming. She tossed and turned for a while until, finally, sleep crept in.

The next morning, Amelia woke early. Pulling open the bed curtains, she arose, pulled on her dressing gown and went to a pair of French doors leading out to a tiny balcony. She opened them and stepped outside. The sun was coming up in the sky, and it looked like it would be a glorious spring day for her wedding. Breathing deeply, she inhaled the aromatic scent of roses and wisteria. Wondering where the flowers were, she looked down and spied a rose arbor in the small garden below. When she had time, she would go exploring.

She would become Mrs. Warren De Winter in a matter of hours. Pin pricks raced up and down her arms at the thought.

Warren told her the night before that he had arranged for them to marry at St. Paul's Cathedral. When she first arrived in London, she took the children for a walk and they'd stumbled upon the cathedral. She had wanted to make the climb to the top. Unfortunately, the children couldn't handle all the stairs. Too bad there would be no time to do it today. She had heard the view of the city from the golden gallery was quite spectacular.

Then realizing she was standing outside in her nightclothes, she stepped back inside her chamber. She would have created a scandal for her betrothed if anyone had seen her. Since she would soon be the wife of a member of the *ton*, she needed to be more circumspect.

With a sigh, she recalled their conversation the night before. While she might grow to love her husband, he made it crystal clear—he would never love her. He believed his heart was buried with his dead wife. How does one compete with the memory of a lost love? Did she even want to try?

Yes, I do.

I deserve love, and I will make it happen.

Warren was already attracted to her, if his lovemaking was any example. While she was somewhat naïve, she didn't think it was lust alone. If that were the case, he would have never insisted on marrying her. He might not realize it, but he needed her love and deep down inside, he wanted it. If it was only sex he had wanted, once he had her, he would have given her the money and sent her on her way. No, he just didn't want to admit that he might be infatuated with her, and if he was infatuated, *that* could turn into love.

Amelia loved children, and Warren had a son. That little boy needed a mother, and if he saw how well she dealt with

Lawrence, that would help her campaign to gain his affection. Between that, and her willingness to warm his bed whenever he desired, she *would* win his heart.

All the incredible feelings she experienced the night before came rushing back. When Warren made love to her, her body sang with a multitude of sensations coursing through her. In fact, thinking of it had her core dripping with need. Lord, she wished he were here right now, so he could fuck her deep and hard as he had last night in the drawing room. Something about the word fuck titillated her. It was dark, forbidden and wicked sounding, and she couldn't wait for him to make love to her again. She never imagined she would like being wicked and wanton, but she did. He had told her she wouldn't get much sleep on her wedding night, and she meant to hold him to his promise.

A knock on the door interrupted her musings, and she called out, "Come in." The maid entered carrying a tray laden with serving dishes. "If that's breakfast, thank you. I'm famished."

Susan set the tray on the table. "Yes, miss. I wasn't sure what ye liked so I brung ye a little bit o' ever'thing. Lady Willhoite told me t' tell ye, she'd be in shortly t' help ye get ready fer th' wedding."

Amelia sat down at the table and took off the dome covering the plate. The freshly baked bread smelled divine, and all the marvelous food made her stomach growl.

"Umm, this looks delicious. Can you pull out my brown dress while I break my fast? I'm aware I don't have much time, but I want to visit my brother and sister before I dress for my wedding."

"Yes, miss. I'll take care o' it."

By the time Amelia came back from seeing the children, Lady Willhoite was waiting for her. "Miss Harrington, we don't have a lot of time. Come, child, sit while the maid fixes your hair."

"I'm sorry I kept you waiting. I needed to check on Justin and Carrie. I visited them late last night and found them crying and in much distress. All this is so new for them. They need reassurance that all is well. They are much better this morning." While they talked, Amelia took her seat and Susan arranged her hair.

By ten of the clock she was dressed and ready. When she looked at her reflection in the cheval mirror, shock rushed through her. The gown Lady Willhoite had selected for her was simply beautiful. The ivory lace gown went well with her complexion and clung to all her curves. For someone not versed in the way to dress a lady's coiffure, Susan did an excellent job with her hair. She had swept it up on the crown of her head and left curls streaming down to her shoulders. While she wasn't vain, she had to admit, she looked lovely. She hoped her future husband would think so.

Lady Willhoite came and stood behind her. "You make a stunning bride. I sent for the veil I wore at my wedding. I want you to wear it. I never had a daughter to pass it down to." Lady Willhoite lifted the delicate lace and tulle from its box and showed it to her.

Amelia gasped, "Oh, my, it's gorgeous. Are you sure you want me to wear it?"

"Certainly. The veil will go well with your gown. I'm so pleased my nephew is getting married. I greatly feared he intended to remain a widower for the rest of his life. Even though we met yesterday, I have a good feeling regarding this marriage. I'm confident you will make him happy. Promise me you will be patient with him."

Amelia had no problem with such a request, because she would need a great deal of patience if she wanted to achieve her goal. "I promise to be a good wife for him and a good mother for his son. Mr. De Winter told me how he lost his first wife. I understand how much he loved her. With time I hope to win his affection, if not his heart. I do have one question for you. As I move among the *ton*, will you help me? My stepmother taught me how to behave in society. However, I've never had the opportunity to use those skills."

As Susan adjusted the lace and tulle veil on Amelia's head, Lady Willhoite replied, "I would be happy to, my dear. You shall do fine. I watched you at dinner last night, and you have everything you need for success. I would venture to say you will cause quite a sensation with the *ton*. Since you will be my niece by marriage, please call me Aunt Bernice."

It thrilled her that his aunt seemed to accept her so readily. She missed having an older woman who could give her advice.

"Only if you'll call me Amelia." Taking one last look at her reflection, she stiffened her spine. "I'm ready."

"Ah...De Winter, left with the countess and her husband. You and I will follow. Come Amelia, let us depart for your wedding."

There it was again. Every time Aunt Bernice said her future husband's name, she hesitated. Suspicion colored her thoughts. Warren De Winter might not be his real name. Why would he hide his identity? When they signed the marriage certificate, she would make sure she noticed how he signed it.

They arrived at St. Paul's with a few minutes to spare. Aunt Bernice led her to the vestibule of the church. As they approached the nave, Amelia's heart pounded and her palms began to sweat. The full impact of what she was getting ready to do hit her in the face. Suddenly, she wasn't as sure of herself as she looked around the magnificent church. The power of God spoke to her in a way that had never happened before and it overpowered her. While she wasn't a particularly religious person, she did have a strong belief in God.

Warren waited for her at the altar, standing in all his wedding finery. He wore a charcoal gray redingote with a silver double-breasted waistcoat, black trousers, and a startling white cravat tied in a Gordian knot around his neck. His dark hair was combed back from a broad forehead and an expression of solemnity graced his handsome face. His golden eyes softened when she drew near. With shaking fingers, she placed her hand in his, and he pulled her to his side when the vicar began reciting the marriage lines.

When it came time to repeat her vows her voice wavered slightly, and she stumbled over some of her lines, but then a peace settled over her and her voice rang out strong and true. No matter how they came together, she meant every word. She would love, honor, cherish and obey this man for the rest of her life. When she finished speaking, and they exchanged rings, the vicar pronounced them husband and wife.

When it became her turn to sign the registry, she carefully read the signature, and it clearly stated Warren Alexander De Winter—Earl of Broadmoor.

Her knees gave way and she swayed. Warren grabbed her and kept her from falling. Her heart thundered in her chest as she stared at him.

"You...you're titled? Why didn't you tell me?"

"I planned to tell you tonight once we were alone, and we had the marriage behind us. I didn't want you to panic when you realized you're the wife of an earl. I forgot about signing the registry. Now isn't the time to discuss this. There are people waiting to meet you. I'm sorry. I thought I was doing the right thing. Does it really make any difference?"

"Of course it makes a difference. This means I'm a countess. I accepted the possibility of being the wife of a younger son, not a peer of the realm. The *ton* will expect me to know things I have never learned."

"Let me ask you this. Would you have turned me down if you had known? Would you have given up the chance at a better life for Justin and Carrie?"

He was right. It wouldn't have made any difference. This was still her one chance to improve their lives and nothing would have kept her from taking it.

"No, I would have still agreed. Nonetheless, if I had known, I would be better prepared."

"I'm sorry. I should have told you. However, we both agree it wouldn't have made a difference. Let us put a brave face on it and go meet our guests. Can you do this for me?"

Amelia warily nodded and slid her hand in his offered arm. She allowed him to lead her down the aisle as she met — her new destiny.

Chapter 5

A gathering of people waited for them at the back of the nave. Warren introduced her to several of his friends, and they chatted for a few minutes. Once the crowd dispersed, he led her over to an older, stunningly beautiful woman, who stood with a gentleman with a slight paunch around his middle. "My dear, this is my mother, the Countess of Ryswick and her husband, Lord Ryswick."

Amelia's knees shook as she curtsied. Warren's hand on her elbow steadied her, keeping her from falling flat on her face. She wasn't normally this clumsy. Her new husband's revelation had her head spinning, to say the least. Her cheeks flushed as she pushed her rioting nerves under a tranquil mask of composure. "It's a pleasure to meet you, Lady Ryswick, Lord Ryswick."

The countess gave her a reassuring smile. "I'm so pleased to make your acquaintance. Ever since I received my son's message, I have looked forward to meeting you. You must be very special if you caught his eye. Please call me mother or if you aren't comfortable with that, Sophie. After all, you're part of our family now."

"I would be honored. My mother died giving birth to me. I had a warm and loving stepmother, but I lost her, along with my father last year."

Sophie regarded her with warm sympathetic eyes. "I'm sorry for your loss. I met your father years ago when I had my coming out. I can see a slight family resemblance. I understand you have a brother and sister. I'm sure they're a great comfort to you."

Warren placed his hand on her arm. "Sorry to interrupt. However, it's time to go to my townhouse for the wedding breakfast. Mother, you can carry on with this discussion there. Will you take Aunt Bernice with you?"

"Of course, it would be our pleasure."

Warren escorted Amelia to the waiting carriage and helped her into the front-facing seat. Once seated beside her, he turned toward her. "As I told you earlier, I'm sorry you found out about my title this abruptly. I should have told you when I asked you to marry me."

She gave him a chilling stare. "Yes, you should have. I'm ill prepared to be a countess." While part of her was thrilled, anxiety raced through her, chilling her to the bone at the thought of what people would expect of her.

"I'm sure you'll handle your duties admirably. My mother will help you, so you need not worry. I'm somewhat of a recluse, especially over the last three years. We'll attend a few parties, and my mother will give a ball to introduce you to society, before we leave for Broadmoor Manor next week. We'll spend most of our time there." The carriage slowed down and pulled to a stop. "Ah, we've arrived. Come, my dear, let us enjoy the festivities my aunt has arranged."

Mrs. Goodall had prepared a sumptuous repast for the wedding breakfast. The chef had created an exquisite wedding cake of such delicacy it stole her breath away. It amazed her that anyone could create such a work of art from icing. She certainly hoped her nerves would calm so she could enjoy all the wonderful food choices.

Her new husband stayed by her side and introduced her to more acquaintances and family. She felt wary of Viscount Rutherford. He eyed her with such intent, it made her feel unclothed. There was no doubt in her mind — he was a rake of the first order.

She dismissed this aggravating thought, because she had other more important things to worry about, such as her new responsibilities. She had an opportunity to talk further with Sophie, and she reassured her that she would indeed help her adjust to her new title, and Aunt Bernice agreed to stay on until they left for Broadmoor. While her duties as a countess worried her, it just made her even more determined to succeed. When she dreamed of marriage in the past she imagined herself married to a steward like her father, or possibly a scholar, never a peer of the realm. Of course, she always learned new things quickly, and after all, her stepmother taught her well. The bigger challenge would be learning how to manage a large household, something she never expected to do.

Once all the guests left, Sophie approached her. "May we go upstairs and see how the children are getting along? I'm sure Lawrence is fine, but I *would* like to check on him before we depart."

"Certainly. I look forward to meeting him, and I can also use the occasion to check on my brother and sister."

When they entered the schoolroom, the children were gathered around a young woman reading a story. Sophie introduced her as her grandson's governess, Miss Hilton. Justin and Carrie ran to her, wrapping their little arms around her. Carrie announced, "Sister, we have a friend."

"I know you do, darling. Would you like to introduce me?" Carrie grabbed her hand and led her over to an adorable little boy. The child had deep red curls floating around his face and golden eyes — so like his father's — which stared up at her with trepidation. Her heart lurched in her chest for this sweet child. Amelia knelt, bringing her eye level with him. "Good afternoon, Lawrence. It's a pleasure to meet you. Please call me Aunt Amelia, while we get to know each other. I hope someday soon you'll want to call me mama, but take all the time you need."

The child looked relieved, so her gentle approach must have reassured him. He gave her a big smile and bowed. "Good day...Aunt Amelia. I'm glad you're going to live here, because you brought me some friends. I like Justin and Carrie. We're having such an enjoyable time together."

"Good. I'm sure we'll get along splendidly. Justin and Carrie miss their friends, so I know they're pleased to have a new one." It relieved her mind greatly that he seemed to accept her so easily. After all, his acceptance and hopefully his love would help her win Warren's affection. After spending a few more minutes talking with the children, she and Sophie left.

When the two of them arrived back downstairs, Sophie and Clayton decided to leave for their townhouse. As her mother-in-law took her leave, she gave Amelia a hug and told her she would return in the morning. Aunt Bernice excused herself and left them alone.

They stood staring at each other, and it felt somewhat awkward. Here she was married to a man she had only met day before yesterday. At last, Warren spoke, breaking the silence. "Mrs. Goodall has moved your things to my suite. If you will come with me, I shall show you our living quarters."

Amelia allowed him to lead her upstairs. When he opened the door to their suite, he stepped back and she entered first. She scanned the chamber, taking in the attractive sitting room. The soft yellow walls matched the furnishings. A set of doors led onto a balcony, overlooking the garden. There was a small French desk sitting against the wall, where she could handle her correspondence, which should increase dramatically now that she was a countess. A sofa with tables on each end sat in front of the fireplace, and she could see herself curled up on it, settling in for a nice long read.

"This room is charming. May I see my bedchamber?"

"Of course." Warren walked across the carpet and opened a door to the right. "This will be your room. I hope you'll be comfortable."

Amelia walked through the door and found the bedchamber blended well with the sitting room. Both areas were feminine, and she wondered where his chambers were. There were two doors on the wall in front of her. She went over and opened one and found a spacious bathing room with a large tub, easily large enough for two people. She closed the door and went to the other one. Here, she found a spacious dressing closet waiting to be filled with all the gowns and dresses she would order tomorrow when Sophie took her shopping. As they moved into the room, she noticed a door on the wall straight ahead.

Warren stepped forward and turned the knob. "Let me show you my chambers."

She followed him through another dressing area filled with clothing. He opened another door and led her to a room similar in size to hers. An enormous bed with a gold counterpane and matching bed curtains stood on a raised dais. The furniture was dark mahogany and much more masculine than what was in her bedchamber.

After giving her a chance to peruse his sleeping quarters, he led her across the room. "Let me show you my personal study."

When they entered, Amelia looked around and found another well-appointed space, matching the color scheme in Warren's bedchamber. "Goodness, these rooms alone are bigger than many houses. I'm sure I'll be quite comfortable."

"Why don't we go back to your bedchamber, and I will show you how to ring for a maid. Susan can assist you for now. My mother will help you find a lady's maid, who will know how to care for your new clothing. I understand Mother is taking you to her modiste tomorrow, so you can select a new wardrobe."

Her skin prickled at the notion of having ball gowns and evening dresses, dinner gowns and day dresses in a multitude of glorious colors. She had always wanted to dress as a lady. "I look forward to it. May I also buy new clothing for my brother and sister? Most of their clothes are too small for them, and I wasn't able to afford new garments."

"Of course, my dear. Buy whatever they need. Oh, and purchase some dolls for Carrie. Since I didn't have any sisters, there aren't any for her to play with. I want all of you to feel at home here."

"You're far too generous, my lord. Thank you ever so much for thinking of my sister. She will be thrilled."

"Any big purchases you make, we can send on to Broadmoor Manor. We will be leaving town in ten days, a few days after the celebration ball Mother is giving for us. I will leave you to your bath now. I shall see you this evening at dinner."

Amelia watched as Warren went back through their dressing rooms. His kindness surprised her, yet it also comforted her. Not only was he going to pay for wardrobes for all of them, he wanted her to purchase dolls. It was so thoughtful of him to think of her sister. Carrie would be ecstatic. How fortunate she was to have met such a considerate gentleman. Oh yes, she would be quite comfortable here.

After her bath, Susan helped her dress for dinner. Aunt Bernice's dressmaker had sent over a dinner gown for her. The lovely peach satin dress with little puffed sleeves which barely capped her upper arms looked stunning. It was the most beautiful gown, other than her wedding dress, she had ever worn. Once she finished getting ready, she went downstairs and entered the drawing room. Abercrombie informed her that Aunt Bernice ordered a tray, so she wouldn't be joining them for dinner.

After the butler left, her gaze landed on a pianoforte placed in front of the large mullioned window. She went over, sat on the piano bench and began to play. It felt good to touch the keys, to hear music fill a room again. Her stepmother had taught her, and playing was one of the things she had missed most when they left their home. Step-Mama had started teaching Carrie before she died, and now, she could carry on. Looking up, she noticed Warren standing in the doorway watching her.

He moved into the room and approached her. "You play well. I enjoy hearing music in the evening. Since I've lived alone for the last three years, I rarely had the opportunity."

He had changed for dinner and was now dressed all in black, except for the sparkling white linen of his cravat. The cut-away redingote fit him snugly and molded to his broad shoulders and muscular arms. Her stomach flip-flopped and the place between her legs grew moist. She couldn't wait for him to take her in his arms. Her cheeks flushed, so she looked down, not wanting him to realize what she was thinking.

While she pushed back her wayward thoughts, Abercrombie entered and announced dinner. Warren escorted her to the dining room and sat her beside him at the table.

"Since Aunt Bernice isn't joining us, we can share an intimate meal." The footmen set out the serving dishes and left after Warren dismissed them. Once they filled their plates, he remarked, "I hope you enjoy lobster. It's one of my favorite dishes, and my chef makes an excellent cream sauce he serves with it."

"I haven't eaten lobster before. The food looks appetizing and smells delicious. I enjoyed meeting your son this afternoon. I suggested he call me Aunt Amelia for now. After he has a chance to get to know me, I hope he'll want to call me mama, if that meets with your approval? He's adorable, and he has your golden eyes. Where did he get the red hair?"

Pain filtered across his face. "I want what is best for my son. If calling you 'Mama' will benefit him, then so be it. My wife...Lucinda had red hair as a child. We were betrothed from birth, so we were always aware that we would marry when we grew up."

Amelia was taken aback. She hadn't realized he had known his wife since they were children. No wonder he had loved her to such a degree. That would make it even more challenging to win his heart, but she wasn't giving up. She had seen desire in his eyes when he looked at her earlier. While lust wasn't love, it was a good place to start.

"You must have many fond memories of your time together as children. I had a wonderful friend while growing up. When Bernard turned eighteen and left for the army, I missed him terribly. We haven't seen each other since."

"That must be difficult for you. I'm sure you miss him."

"Yes, I do. It *is* quite difficult, since we were as close as a brother and sister. Since it's inappropriate for a young lady to correspond with a gentleman, I have to depend on his mother for news. Bernard has done well from what she has told me and is now a Captain."

Warren sat his wine glass down. "It's good to have friends growing up. Lucinda was two years younger than I, and when I went away to school, I made friends with Mallory. I went through a stage where I didn't want to spend time with her. At times, I was quite mean to Lucinda when she tried to tag along. All that changed when I finished my time at Oxford, and we were wed. You've mentioned your stepmother several times. I gather you were close."

"Oh, my, yes, very close. Since my father raised me, I was quite a hoyden, and much more inclined to play with soldiers than dolls. That's why Bernard and I were so close. However, my stepmother did teach me how to act as a lady. What about you? When did you lose your father?"

"Ten years ago. He died a few months after I turned eighteen. Lord Ryswick was one of the trustees my father appointed, in case he died before I reached my majority. He helped me adjust to the duties of the earldom at such a young age. He also kept me grounded. That way I didn't fall into the rakish ways of my friend, Mallory."

"I'm glad you had him to count on. It must have been difficult to lose your father. May I ask how Lord Ryswick came to be married to your mother?"

"Since Lord Ryswick spent so much time at my estate helping me, he had the opportunity to fall in love with her. At first, my mother didn't return his regard. Eventually he won her over, and they have a wonderful marriage."

"They do *seem* happy, and I like both of them already." With skepticism in her tone, she confessed, "I know Lord Rutherford is your best friend, but I need to tell you I didn't care for him very much. I sensed his rakish attitude as soon as I met him. I don't think he has much respect for women."

"You're right, he doesn't. Mallory lost his parents when he was a small child, and since he didn't get along well with his guardian, he spent holidays with me. His aunt treated him terribly while he grew up, and his uncle didn't treat him much better. That's why he spent such a great deal of time with me. I don't agree with many of my friend's activities, nevertheless, he's always been a good friend. I can promise you this, he would never hurt you."

"I'll take your word on that. It was nice of your parents to let him join you on your holidays and summers." Sensing it was important to him, she told him, "All right, I shall reserve judgment until I have the opportunity to get to know him."

"It's getting late, why don't we retire for the evening? I can think of more enjoyable things for us to do than talking."

Giving her a burning look, he stood and helped her from her seat, then escorted her upstairs to her bedchamber.

Once Susan helped her undress and took her hair down, Amelia sent her off to her bed. It still felt uncomfortable having someone help her, but her new gowns were impossible for her to remove on her own, and it did feel nice having the girl brush her hair every night. She went over and sat in the chair by the empty hearth. Her heart thumped in her chest. She lifted her trembling hand to her forehead and felt light beads of perspiration. It was such a warm evening she pushed the drapes to the side and checked the window, making sure it was open. Of course, nerves more than the heat caused her to sweat. She stood and let the cool spring breeze caress her skin as the scent of roses drifted in. Determined to start her plan to win Warren's love tonight, she eagerly waited for him to arrive.

There was a light tap on her dressing room door. It opened and there stood her husband in all his masculine beauty. He looked so handsome with his hair still damp from his bath. The scent of his bergamot cologne wrapped around her, leaving her dizzy with desire as it shot to the center of her pleasure. His broad muscular chest was hidden beneath a dark blue silk dressing gown and white lawn nightshirt. She wished he didn't have on the nightshirt, so she could have seen what must be a magnificent chest. Remembering the pleasure she would soon enjoy had her nether regions clenching.

She met his smoldering gaze boldly. This wasn't the time for shy, unassuming behavior. She needed to be brazen, a siren bent on seduction, so she could capture his full attention. Taking a step forward, Amelia allowed her dressing gown to slip off her shoulders, showing the thin straps of her night rail. She took several more steps forward, bringing her closer to him.

His nostrils flared as he glimpsed her cleavage. Taking the last step, he pulled her into his arms. "Damn, you're beautiful. I want—no I need—to see all of you. Take off your night rail."

She stepped back, untied the sash and let her dressing gown slip to the floor, then reached down and slowly pulled up her night rail an inch at a time while gazing seductively into his eyes. She pulled the wispy slip of a gown off and let it drop to the floor in a puddle of black silk. Her heart thundered when he pulled her back into his muscular arms. His lips swooped down, covering hers as his tongue dove into the deep recesses of her mouth. Her tongue met his, dueling for domination. Chills raced through her as Warren reached up and fondled her naked breast. His very touch had her nipples drawing up into tight buds, causing them to ache with need.

"Your nipples are so luscious. They look like delicious little berries, ready for me to devour." Dropping his head, he sucked one into his mouth, sending her whirling as he sucked furiously on her nipple. He scooped her up, carried her over to the bed and dropped her in the center, then stepped back. He reached into the pocket of his dressing gown and pulled out three red silk scarves. "I'm going to blindfold you and tie you up."

"Why? I want to see you and touch you, as you..." She hesitated before using the naughty word he had taught her, "fuck me."

"Remember, I don't want to be touched. I can't take my clothes off unless you're blindfolded and your hands tied." In a compelling voice, he demanded, "Do this for me."

Why didn't he want her to touch him? This didn't make any sense. However, if it was that important to him she would comply. She hoped someday soon he would trust her enough to tell her why he didn't like being touched. With her desire at a fever pitch, she would have agreed to anything. She craved the feel of his hands on her body, bringing her fulfillment.

"As you wish, my lord."

"Now, now...no need for formality in the bedchamber. When we're alone, use my given name."

"Certainly...Warren."

Settling back against the sheets, she closed her eyes as he tied one of the silk scarves around her head. Her breath caught as he lifted her wrist and tied it to the bedpost. While he did this she continued wondering why this seemed of such importance to him. While a little naïve, she didn't think it normal for him to want to do this to her. Since her arousal at this point had increased ten-fold, she wouldn't worry over it right now. Once both of her wrists were secured, he moved away. She laid still all a quiver, awaiting his touch. She heard the rustle of clothing, as he disrobed. When he joined her, fingers trailed down her sides, sending tingles cascading through her.

The burn of desire rushed to her feminine core, that special place she had only now realized she possessed. Her breathing grew shallow as Warren left a trail of hot, wet kisses down her belly, and on to her pubic area, where he licked her womanly flesh. It sent a thousand pinpricks rushing to her nether region.

"Ah, you have the most delicious pussy. I could nibble on you all night. Your sweet honey is dripping from your body." At his naughty words, her cheeks flushed and her center tightened. Amelia couldn't control herself any longer. She writhed and twisted, trying to move closer to his silken tongue. He breathed deeply as he crooned, "Hmm, I love the scent of your arousal."

Just when she thought she couldn't take any more, his tongue invaded her body, sending her flying over the edge into bliss. While still reeling from all the marvelous sensations coursing through her body, he covered her and thrust deep inside her, pumping his manly flesh in over and over, faster and deeper, each time filling her fuller than before. Even though her hands were tied, she wanted to take part in their lovemaking. Instead of lying passive, she wrapped her legs around his hips, drawing him in, causing friction, sending frissons of delight scattering along her spine. The tension built yet again, and as he shouted out her name, his essence poured into her, and she splintered into a million tiny pieces.

Stunned at the magnitude of what had happened to her, she tried to catch her breath and allow her heartbeat to slow. A great sense of euphoria swept over her. Never in a thousand years would she have expected to feel such ecstasy. She listened while Warren pulled his nightshirt back on and turned out the bedside lamp. After he untied her wrists and took off the blindfold, at first, it was inky black. Slowly, her eyes adjusted, and she saw his shadowy form crawl into bed with her.

Pulling her to him, he murmured, "Thank you, my dear."

"No, thank you, for such an incredible night. I never imagined lovemaking could be this pleasurable. Can I ask you something?"

"Of course."

"Why don't you like me touching you?"

Warren hesitated before he spoke. "I know I told you about the fire, and that I nearly died. My upper torso and arms were badly burned. The scars are horrendous — they would repulse you. I haven't allowed anyone to see me or touch me in three years. I suppose I could keep my nightshirt on while we make love."

"I enjoy the feel of your skin touching mine. Why don't you let me see you? I'm sure it's not as bad as you think. We're always our own worst critic. At least think about it."

"I shall consider it, but I make no promises. Enough talk, we need some sleep. If I know my mother, your day will be full tomorrow."

As she lay there, Warren stroked her hair and she found it soothing. His breathing grew heavy and deep, and she knew he had fallen asleep. She pondered all he had told her. How difficult it must be for him to live with those scars. Amelia wanted to help him overcome his revulsion, and she hoped with time she would be able to. She grew drowsy and closed her eyes, falling fast asleep as she dreamed of the day when he would cast off the bonds holding him and allow himself the freedom to live again.

Chapter 6

Warren awoke with his wife spooned against his body. His stiff erection nestled against the cleft of her delightfully, rounded ass. Blood surged through his prick, making it stiff as a pike. He had to take her again. Passion for this woman was almost frightening in its intensity. He nuzzled her shoulder and kissed the base of her neck. Her auburn curls were in the way, and he brushed them to the side as he continued to nibble on her neck and shoulders.

Sighing, she purred, "Umm that feels nice."

"I need you again, wife. There's nothing like a good rousing romp in the morning. Get on your hands and knees. I want to ride you from behind." She gave him a quizzical look but did what he asked and presented her delectable rump to him. He stroked her soft skin and gave her derriere a light pat. "Spread your legs further apart."

Moving in, he reached down and spread her luscious pink folds. Finding her clitoris, he massaged it with his fingers. Soon, he had her cunt dripping wet and ready. He hastily pushed the nightshirt out of the way. Taking his bulging erection, he rubbed her love juices over it. Pleasure raised a fever pitch in him, and he drove deep inside her sheath. Waves of sensations rushed through the nerve endings of his cock to the point where he feared he would spend sooner than he wanted. Determined to enjoy her beguiling cunny as long as possible, he reined in his passions and stroked in and out slowly, letting the tension build. His movements sped up as flesh slapped against flesh with each thrust. Her wet heat surrounded him. The muscles in his neck tensed and his arms shook as he fought to hold off his climax until she was there with him.

When Amelia made soft mewling sounds, and moved her hips, trying to get closer, he sensed she was near to her own release. Slipping a hand around her belly, he gently pinched her love bud, and her pulsing portal clenched around him, sending him over the edge into the most fierce climax he could ever remember having. He pulled out, and rolled onto the bed, to give his heart a chance to slow down and allow his breathing to return to normal. "Sweetheart, now *that* is the way to greet the morning. I hope I wasn't too rough, but I needed you in the worst way. I don't think I'll ever get tired of fucking you."

She smiled over at him with a sated look on her face. "So, you enjoy my...uh, pussy. I never knew what to call that part of my body before. What do you call your man part?"

"Actually the correct name for it is penis. I usually refer to it as my cock or my prick. Sometimes men will give it a name. I do believe you enjoy me talking dirty to you."

Even though she blushed furiously, she met his gaze. "I find it quite arousing. I want to learn everything about…fucking. I do love it when you take me hard and deep. I think I enjoyed you entering me from behind. Are there other positions?"

"Oh, yes, there are plenty, and we will explore all of them at another time. I need to get up, because I have a meeting with my secretary, Humphries, this morning. Some of my peers are pushing me to help them keep a bill from passing in Parliament. I took my seat when I came of age. However, I haven't participated for the last three years." Warren climbed out of the bed, pulled on his dressing gown and smiled down at her.

Looking up at him, she remarked, "If I were a man, I would love being a Member of Parliament. Think of the good you could do. My father was interested in politics. He would have loved to run for the House of Commons. Since he had to take care of me, he never stood for office, even though Lord Hollingsworth would have supported him."

"I did find it challenging, until I lost Lucinda. I stopped going to London for the sessions and turned my back on all the things I used to enjoy. All my focus was on making sure I left a strong legacy for my son when I die. None of us know when we are going to leave this life. Losing Lucinda taught me that."

"I can understand why it might be difficult to go on living." She hesitated a moment, before continuing, as if worried he would not like her next comment. He tensed while he waited for her to speak. "I'm sure Lucinda would want you to enjoy life. I agree with what you said a moment ago, none of us know how long we have on this earth, and we need to make the best of it. Please let your grief go, so you can live again."

His heart seized when he thought of his darling Lucinda. Guilt swept through him like a raging storm. He couldn't speak of her with Amelia. It would betray her memory to do so. He would *not* let this new wife enter his heart. "I can tell you want me to love you. That shall not happen. I have to go. You need to remember what I told you when I asked you to marry me and not badger me about love."

Looking taken aback and hurt, she declared with a sharp tone, "I never mentioned love. All I asked is that you start living the life God has given you, instead of having one foot in the grave. Please leave. I need to dress, and go see my brother and sister."

Warren walked over to the door, jerked it open and stomped from the room, slamming the door behind him. Once in his room, he took a deep breath. Rage coursed through his body, rolling through him like a tidal wave.

What does she know about the pain I feel?

Why did I think I needed to marry her?

She was little better than a common doxy. After all, Amelia had willingly agreed to go with him. She knew he assumed she was a whore, but she went with him with the sole purpose of laying with him for money. And then, she even bargained with him for that absurd sum of ten pounds. It was all her fault, and now, he was stuck with her.

He went to the bathing room, slinging his nightshirt off and splashed water on his face. He thought he had grown resigned to this marriage and that it would be tolerable. Now, it would be a living hell. The last thing he wanted or needed was a wife telling him what to do or how to feel. He would need to stay away from her during the day. No, he would keep their interaction to the bedchamber and no more sleeping with her all night. In the future, he would go to her, do his business and leave.

Damnation. Had he actually told her about the fire and what it did to him? Even told her about the hideous scars, something he never talked about? He didn't owe her an explanation. To top it all off, he'd told her he would consider letting her see them. Devil take it. It would be a cold day in hell before he let that happen! His valet entered in response to his summons.

While he continued to fume, Hendricks shaved him, but in his agitated state he moved, and his valet almost nicked him. It would have been his fault if Hendricks had cut him, so he didn't reprimand the man. He craved the peace of Broadmoor Manor, but he had ten days before he could find solace — thanks to his mother, and the worst part of it — he would have to take her with him.

After Warren finished the meeting with his secretary, he made his way to Gentleman Jackson's gym where he met Mallory for a bruising round of fisticuffs. It was what he needed to work off some steam over what happened that morning with Amelia. When they finished the match, they both agreed to meet again at their club for luncheon.

While dining on rare roast beef and roasted potatoes, Mallory asked, "How goes it with your marriage, my friend? You seem tense and that was one hell of a match you gave me this morning. I'll wear this shiner for a week."

Warren grinned over at him. "Sorry. You need to learn to avoid my right hook. As far as my marriage goes, its going as well as any marriage of convenience does. Amelia's off shopping with my mother for a new wardrobe, this morning. I'm sure it will set me back a few quid. You need to remember. I married her to give my son a mother, and of course to have her warm my bed. That part is going *very* well."

"Then why are you so tense today?"

"I guess I'm too used to being alone. A wife's a damned nuisance. She's already trying to influence me on matters that are none of her concern."

"Such as?"

He didn't want to discuss his dealings with his wife, but his friend wouldn't let this drop until he told him something. "I know she wants me to fall in love with her and that's *not* going to happen."

"Women always expect love. You should have realized that. Albeit, it *is* time you moved on with your life. I know how much you loved Lucinda, however she's gone, and she's not coming back. It's time you started living again. You have lived the life of a recluse. You haven't participated in any sessions in Parliament since Lucinda died, nor have you attended any parties, staying holed up at Broadmoor Manor all year long. Listen, we need your vote on this upcoming bill the Tories are trying to push down our throats."

Relieved to get the topic off his wife, he jumped on this issue. "I met with my secretary this morning, and I have decided to lend my support. I will be there when the vote comes up."

"Well done, my friend. We need all the votes we can get. Now, why don't you come with me to Tattersall's? There's a sweet going pair I'm thinking of buying for my new racing curricle. Lord Halsey took a huge loss at the tables the other night and has no choice. He has to sell them. I think I'll be able to purchase the pair for less than five hundred guineas, which would be an incredible deal."

Warren spent the rest of the afternoon with Mallory, and by the time he returned home, he was in a much better frame of mind. At least he could avoid being alone with Amelia at dinner tonight, because his mother and Clayton would be joining them.

After he finished dressing, he joined everyone in the drawing room. Fortunately, his mother and Clayton arrived, so thank God he could avoid spending time alone with her. Shortly after he entered, Aunt Bernice came into the room and Abercrombie announced dinner.

The conversation at the table, centered on Amelia's shopping expedition. From what he gathered, it had been a success. The modiste promised to have several of her gowns ready by Saturday. That way she would have something appropriate for the opera. It would be his wife's first appearance before the *ton*. While his mother wanted her seen, she wanted her formal presentation to occur at their celebration ball on Monday night.

When Warren and Clayton rejoined the ladies, after enjoying their port and cigars, Amelia entertained them by playing the pianoforte and singing. She had an enchanting, light, lyric soprano voice and her singing was much more accomplished than he would have expected. In fact, it quite astonished him. Her stepmother had taught her well. Over all, it was a relaxing evening and his mother and Clayton left at ten. After they departed, Warren used the excuse that he needed to go over something his secretary left for him and bid Amelia and his aunt goodnight.

He decided to forgo bed play tonight. That way he could further distance himself from Amelia. After going over the reports Humphries had left, he selected a book and spent several hours reading and drinking brandy. The clock on the mantle chimed the one o'clock hour. Feeling a trifle foxed, he went upstairs to bed.

The next five days went well. He avoided almost all contact with his wife, so he felt much more grounded again. While he missed the sex, he didn't miss her questions.

He enjoyed attending Parliament and had reconnected with several of his friends. Seeing old friends made him realize how much he missed the camaraderie he shared with them. The challenge was still there, and he had joined in on several of the debates. A well-thought out argument debated and won always gave him a great deal of satisfaction. While he hated to admit it, both Amelia and Mallory were right, it was time he let go of some of his grief.

Each morning that week, he took Lawrence for a ride in the park, and all his son could talk about was his new friends. At least something good came from his marriage. The boy seemed thrilled to have friends to play with. Justin and Carrie had joined him in his studies, and that was going well, from all he heard. He also appeared to adore Amelia and was now calling her mama. While it pained him to think of his son calling her by such an intimate title, it was best for Lawrence. After all, one of the benefits he hoped to achieve with this marriage was a loving mother for his son.

Since they were attending the opera that evening, there was no way he could avoid spending time with Amelia. At least he would have his mother as a buffer and wouldn't be alone with her. After dressing in evening clothes, he joined Amelia and his aunt in the drawing room. "Good evening, ladies. Are you looking forward to the opera tonight?"

Amelia gave him a brilliant smile, beaming with enthusiasm. "Oh, yes, I have never been to the opera, though I am familiar with the music from *Don Giovanni*. I know I shall enjoy it. My favorite aria is *Batti, Batti o Bel Masetto*. It's good for my vocal range."

Warren was impressed to find her familiar with the opera, since the composition of Mozart's had only been introduced last year. He hadn't expected to have that in common with her. "You must perform it for me sometime. If we are going to arrive on time, I suggest we dine, and then we can be on our way."

When they arrived at Covent Gardens, Warren found himself watching Amelia's reaction to the famous Royal Opera House. Her warm hazel eyes filled with awe as they made their way to their box. The *ton* filled the house to capacity, with this being the first performance of *'Don Giovanni'* in London.

She had on one of her new evening gowns and it enticed him, to say the least. Her plump tits were practically spilling out of the bodice of her gown. His shaft grew hard as stone as he remembered taking one of her berry-hued nipples into his mouth. Desire coursed through his veins. To hell with it, he'd have her tonight. After all, that was another one of the benefits of this marriage. Why should he deny himself?

When they returned home from the performance that night, he would visit her bed. He'd just need to use caution. No conversation was needed for what he had in mind. Then he would leave after he finished fucking her. If he didn't sleep with her, there would be no chance of a conversation the next morning. Settling in his seat, he glanced down and noticed Mallory in the pit. There was no doubt in his mind what his friend had planned for the evening. A new ballet dancer had caught Mallory's eye, and he was offering her carte blanche.

As the soprano, playing Zerlina, performed the aria Amelia told him was her favorite, she sang along in hushed tones. While darkness surrounded him, Warren could still see the rapture on her beautiful face. He was determined to see even more rapture on her lovely countenance later, when he threw her into the throes of passion. Perhaps he would leave the blindfold off tonight, that way he could watch her expression as he brought her to climax.

By this time, his cock pressed against the buttons on his breeches. All these sexual images running through his mind weren't helping. He needed to remove himself from his wife's presence, or he would end up ravishing her in front of his mother and God knows who else. Once the first act ended, he excused himself. He went down to the pit and located Mallory. "So, which ballet dancer is Suzette?"

"She's the dark haired one in the front. She has given me every indication she will accept my offer, so the contract is in my pocket. I'm taking her to dinner after the performance, and after that, I shall spend the rest of the night fucking her hard and long. In fact, I may keep her in my bed for the next two days. I would probably keep her there longer, but alas, we have the vote on Monday afternoon. Can we still count on your vote?"

"Of course. It would be an atrocity if the bill goes through. Do you think we have enough support to keep it from passing?"

Mallory gave him a smug smile. "Definitely. Since the Duke of Rutland joined us, he's brought several others with him, and with your vote, we can keep it from making it through the house."

The theater grew dim as the ushers blew out some of the wall sconces. "I need to return to my box. Enjoy yourself tonight. I shall see you on Monday, my friend." And with a parting clap on Mallory's shoulder, he went back to his box.

When they arrived back at the house, Warren escorted Amelia to her room. He didn't mention visiting her, because he hoped to catch her off guard. He would give her enough time to get in bed, and then he would join her. He wanted to time it so he entered her room as she was falling asleep. If she was drowsy, she might not say anything when he didn't tie her up.

Later that evening, he entered her chamber, and his timing was perfect. Amelia looked over at him with sleep-filled eyes. In a husky voice, he murmured, "I thought I would join you tonight." Since he didn't want to blindfold her or tie her up, he left the nightshirt on. Pulling back the covers, he slid between the sheets. He pulled her into his embrace and gave her a bruising kiss to distract her.

Soon he had her purring. He dispensed with her night rail and rained kisses from her mouth to her breast. His head felt dizzy with the scent of her sweet smelling body. Taking her turgid nipple into his mouth, he sucked hard, yet not enough to cause pain, only pleasure, while his hands roamed down to her honey pot.

He parted her thighs and dipped a finger into her and found her wet and ready. Stroking her, he pushed a second finger in while he toyed with her clitoris using his thumb. Her inner muscles clenched around his fingers and he sensed she was close to climaxing. He crawled up her body and devoured her mouth as he plunged into her. In and out, he pumped, ever faster and deeper. The thrill of it rippled through his veins. Amelia made a high keening sound as her body jerked with the force of her climax, driving him into an overpowering one of his own. His essence filled her channel as he lost all control and shouted out her name.

His arms no longer held him up and he slumped on top of her, burying his face in the curve of her neck, feeling supremely sated. He had missed this a great deal. Holding her close, he savored the feel of her warm, soft body. Her arms clasped his neck and Amelia let out a deep sigh as she kissed his shoulder through his nightshirt. He could lay here forever, breathing in her tantalizing scent of jasmine and lavender.

"I'm glad you came to me tonight," she murmured. "I have missed this so much. Please don't stay away from my bed again."

"Believe me, I couldn't even if I wanted to, which I don't. You've started a fire in me that only you can appease."

"Well, good. You promised to show me other ways to…fuck, and I mean to hold you to it."

Amelia hesitated whenever she used the word fuck and he found it vastly entertaining. He smothered a laugh. "It will be my pleasure, my dear."

And he did exactly that. He made love to her long and hard most of the night and into the wee hours of the morning, Exhausted, she fell asleep. Keeping true to his plan, Warren slid out of her arms. He stood there watching as she curled up around his pillow, and continued sleeping. Part of him wanted to crawl back in bed, but it would not be wise, so he turned around and went back to his lonely room.

Chapter 7

Amelia heard the door close, thus disturbing the euphoric afterglow of the most amazing sex she had experienced so far. She couldn't deceive herself—Warren left her bed to keep from falling asleep with her. Obviously, he didn't want the intimacy of them waking up together in the morning. At least he *had* come to her, and he hadn't insisted on blindfolding her *or* tying her up. That was a start. How could she gain his affection if he refused to spend any time with her during waking hours? Look at tonight. He waited until she was almost asleep before coming to her bed.

Snuggling up against his pillow, she breathed in the scent of his cologne and an earthier scent of musk that was all his own. Sexual arousal tightened in her inner core and she sighed. She still wanted him, even though they only finished making love moments ago. No, they hadn't made love—he had fucked her, as he called it. There were no tender emotions from him.

Amelia longed for a time when he would gather her in his arms because he loved her, and *not* just because he wanted to fuck her. Well, wishing wouldn't make it happen.

She needed to figure out how to make him spend time with her during the day. Perhaps — yes, that might work. Tomorrow, she would go to his study after church and suggest they take the children on a picnic. That would be a way to see him during daylight hours. Pleased with her idea, she closed her eyes and let sleep take her away.

When Amelia awoke the next morning, she rushed through her morning ablutions, since she'd overslept. Her maid tried to wake her several times, but she'd had a difficult time waking up, after tossing and turning most of the night, worried over how to get Warren to spend more time with her — outside of the bedchamber. Rushing down the stairs, she found Warren and Aunt Bernice impatiently waiting for her. "I'm sorry I'm late. I overslept."

With a frown on his face, Warren bit out, "Never mind that now. We need to hurry, so we aren't late." Offering her his arm, he led her to the waiting carriage with Aunt Bernice following on their heels. At least something went right, the sun shone brightly and a warm spring breeze stirred the air. Warren still looked irritated and didn't say anything on the entire ride to the church.

Amelia normally took the children with her when she went to services. Obviously that wasn't a practice among the *ton*, since there were very few young children there. While they entered one of the back pews, she looked around, and saw several people she'd been introduced to the night before during intermission at the opera. Sophie and Clayton sat several pews ahead of them, and she waved as they took their seats. Sophie gave a slight shake of her head. Oh dear, evidently, she shouldn't have waved.

She settled in her seat and turned toward the pulpit, where the priest stood, ready to start the mass. The sermon was quite good, all about God's forgiveness. She hated when the priest warned about sin and everlasting hellfire if one didn't mend one's ways. Amelia believed much more could be accomplished by focusing on God's love and the need to help each other, than on avoiding sin and evil in the world.

After mass, they made their way outside and joined Sophie and Clayton on the steps. Sophie hugged her. "Are you looking forward to the ball tomorrow night?"

The thought of her first ball sent a thrill of anticipation racing through her. It was all she could do to contain her excitement and keep her tone even. "Oh, Yes, ever so much. I'm sure it will be delightful. It's so kind of you to do this for me. Do you know how many people are attending?"

"I sent out two hundred invitations, and I received one hundred and eighty back accepting. There should be quite a crush."

Visions of all the women in their glittering ball gowns swirling around the dance floor in the arms of handsome gentlemen danced through her head. Her stepmother had taught her the minuet and the cotillion along with the usual country dances and of course, the quadrille and the waltz. Those two had only become popular the last few years. She couldn't wait to participate in it all. Thinking of Warren's arms around her as they waltzed across the ballroom caused goose bumps to rise all along her arms and shoulders.

Warren interrupted before she could answer Sophie. "Here's our carriage. We don't want to hold up traffic. I suggest we continue this discussion back at the townhouse. Mother, you and Clayton are coming for luncheon, aren't you?"

"Of course, darling. We shall meet you there shortly."

A weight heavier than a gigantic stone fell into the pit of Amelia's stomach. If Sophie and Clayton were coming for luncheon, she wouldn't be able to talk him into going on the picnic with the children. And there was no chance of one tomorrow, since he would be spending the afternoon in Parliament. She had the worst misfortune in the world. At the rate she was going, she'd be old and gray before she had a chance to earn Warren's love.

All she could hope for was that when they arrived at Broadmoor Manor, she would be able to persuade him to spend time with her there. Surely there would be plenty of time if he wasn't in Parliament three times a week and off to Gentleman Jackson's gym every morning with his friend, Mallory. Even on the days Parliament didn't sit, Warren managed to avoid her. She was determined to change that when they arrived in the country. Never one to give up, she would continue to wage war on winning her husband's affection.

When they arrived at the townhouse everyone entered together. Abercrombie announced luncheon, and they went into the dining room. Sophie picked up their conversation where they had left it and told her some useful information regarding several members of the *ton*, which would help her at the ball the following evening. Over all, it was a pleasant meal, only Amelia would have preferred to have Warren to herself.

Once everyone finished eating, Sophie asked, "Amelia, can we go upstairs? I want to spend some time with Lawrence, and of course I would like to get to know your brother and sister.

They're adorable children. They must take after your stepmother because I see very little resemblance to you."

"They have her blonde hair. However their blue eyes are like my father's. I resemble my mother for the most part." Amelia laughed as she told her, "I do have my father's stubborn chin." She stood. "Please follow me. I'm sure the children would love to see you."

They spent an hour with the children. Sophie read them a story, and Carrie listened spellbound at the countess's every word. For such a young child, she certainly had a fascination for the written word. She gave Amelia a story she had written and the imagination the child showed actually astonished her. It pleased her when Sophie treated Justin and Carrie with as much warmth and kindness as she showered on her grandson.

After Sophie and Clayton left, Warren excused himself and went to his study. Aunt Bernice told her she needed a nap and went upstairs. Amelia stood there debating. While too late for a picnic, they could still take the children to the park. Determined to engage him in a meaningful conversation, she took a deep breath to steady her nerves and went down the hall to the study and knocked.

Warren's smooth baritone voice called out, "Enter." He looked up when she stepped into the room. He motioned her forward. "Did you need something, my dear?"

"Since it's such a lovely spring day, I thought we might take the children to Hyde Park. I think it's a good idea for Lawrence to see us together. While he has taken to me well, seeing us together can't hurt."

Amelia waited for him to respond. "I suppose we could take them," he hesitated a moment, "I can see your point. I'll order the barouche while you get the children."

She hurried upstairs before Warren had a chance to change his mind. When she entered the schoolroom, the children looked up from their play. Carrie ran to her. "Oh, Sister, I'm glad you came back. We are all quite bored." Waving her hand around, she included Justin and Lawrence in her statement. "Since it's such a splendid day, do you think we can go outside?"

"That's why I'm here. Lord Broadmoor has agreed to take us to the park. Follow me, and we can join him outside."

Lawrence jumped up and piped in, "Do you think we can go to the Serpentine, so we can sail our boats?"

"I don't see why not. Grab them and come along."

The children ran to the shelves and gathered up their brightly colored sailboats. By the time they made it outside, Warren waited for them by the carriage. Lawrence raced to his father's side. "Can we go to the Serpentine and sail our boats, Papa?"

Giving his son a quick hug, he told him, "I think we can do that. I see you have them ready to launch. Come, my young lads and of course, ladies, climb in and we shall be off."

The children clambered in, and Warren offered his hand to Amelia. Smiling, she put her hand in his and electricity shot up her arm at the contact, and that was with their gloves on. After she took her seat, he climbed in, taking the seat next to his son.

Since the traffic to Hyde Park was heavy, the drive took longer than usual. After directing the coachman to the lake, Warren helped her out, while the children raced out of the other side of the carriage with their sailboats in hand. Amelia laughed. "They're certainly in a hurry. Shall we join them before they have a chance to find trouble?"

"Of course, my dear." When he offered his arm, she slid her hand through the crook of his elbow, and they made their way to the lake. Lawrence knelt by the edge and set his boat in the water. Justin did the same thing and so did Carrie. Once all three youngsters had their boats in the water, they clapped their hands and shouts of joy rang out when the warm spring breeze puffed out the tiny sails. They raced along the bank of the lake.

They stepped quickly to keep up with the children. While they played, Amelia smiled up at him. "Thank you for bringing us. My brother and sister are having a delightful time, Lawrence as well. I had hoped we could bring them on a picnic, but with your mother and Clayton coming for luncheon, that couldn't happen."

At this point the children crowded around one of the boats that had capsized. Lawrence waded in to retrieve it before it floated away. "Lawrence," Warren called out, "it's time to take the boats out. The wind is picking up, and you don't want to get any wetter." Looking down at Amelia, he informed her, "The sky is getting dark. I do believe there's a storm approaching. We may be sorry we brought the barouche. We will probably be soaked by the time we arrive back at the house."

"Oh, dear, I hoped we could talk. You stay so busy with Parliament, we haven't had a chance to have a decent conversation all week. I'm sure you will be glad when the vote is taken tomorrow. Are we still leaving for Broadmoor Manor on Friday?"

The wind grabbed the brim of Amelia's bonnet, and it was all she could do to keep it from blowing off. The heavens opened up and rain came slashing down upon them. Warren released her arm and yelled, "Bring the children while I help the coachman put the top up on the barouche. We can finish our discussion when we arrive back at the house."

By the time she gathered up the children and got them back to the carriage, everyone was drenched. The top wasn't designed for protection from weather turned foul. The temperature had dropped drastically. Cold wind blew through the carriage, and the children huddled together shivering.

At least the traffic had cleared out, and they traveled along Upper Grosvenor Street without mishap to Grosvenor Square where the townhouse was located. Amelia rushed the children inside, and together with Warren, returned them to the schoolroom. Once the children were settled he escorted her to her room. "You need to remove those wet clothes. I'll ring for your maid. Since I promised we would talk, I will meet you in your sitting room in fifteen minutes, and we can continue our conversation."

"Very good, my lord. I shall see you in a bit." She rushed into her bedchamber, and removed her wet clothes. Her maid answered her husband's summons, and after she had changed and sent Susan away, she went to her sitting room. Since Warren wasn't there yet, she took a seat by the hearth, where someone had started a fire to take the chill out of the room. It was truly amazing how cold it had become so quickly.

While she waited for her husband to join her, her heart fluttered as she thought about spending time with him. It pleased her tremendously that he agreed to continue their discussion. Perhaps they could actually have a private conversation for a change. She heard a knock. The door opened and Warren entered the room.

He looked magnificent, standing in the doorway with his hair still damp from the rain. That one stubborn lock fell down on his broad forehead. Her hands itched to brush it from his face, but if she touched him, it would probably lead to them making love. As much as she desired him, they needed to talk. Besides, it was daytime and lovemaking was best left to the night. Although her husband didn't feel any hesitancy regarding making love during the day, as their episode in the study flitted across her mind. Her womanly flesh grew wet remembering how he had taken her on his desk.

Warren joined her on the sofa. "That rain storm certainly came up quickly. I hope none of the children catch a cold. Now where were we? Ah, yes, you asked if we were still leaving on Friday. To answer your question, yes."

"I look forward to seeing Broadmoor Manor. I imagine it's quite extensive. How large an estate is it?"

Stretching his arm, he laid it across the back of the sofa. It brushed her shoulders and chills raced along her skin from having a part of his body so close to hers. It made it hard to concentrate on their conversation, but she was determined to keep wayward thoughts out of her mind as he described his home.

"Broadmoor Manor isn't a large estate, compared to some of my peers, only around five thousand acres. The land is fertile and most of it is planted with barley and wheat. A portion of my estate is set aside for dairy farming, which means we have ample supplies of fresh dairy products. There's a lake not too terribly far from the manor house. I spent a great deal of time swimming and fishing there as a young lad. The gardens are extensive around the house and quite magnificent."

"It sounds wonderful. I used to roam Lord Hollingsworth's lands. He allowed me the use of one of the horses from his stables, and Bernard and I would ride for hours most days. I love horses, and I'm quite skilled at riding. Do you keep a good stable?"

Amelia waited with bated breath. She had missed riding a great deal during the last eight months, so she certainly hoped he did.

"Yes, I do. I also do some horse breeding. I'm pleased you ride. I have a gentle, yet spirited mare that will be perfect for you. You may have her for your riding pleasure. I'm sure you will find Genevieve to your liking."

"Oh, thank you. I promise to take good care of her. I have never had a mount of my own. It's very generous of you, my lord." So pleased, she reached up and kissed his cheek. Warren pulled her to him and passionately devoured her lips. Desire flared, and she returned his kiss, seeking to get as close to him as possible. All thought of keeping her passions in check fled as she gave herself up to the glory of his kiss.

Pleasure thrummed through every muscle when he cupped her breast through her gown. Warren pulled down her bodice and chemise, baring her naked breasts as he swooped down and tugged one of her tumescent nipples into the depths of his wicked mouth. His hand traveled down to the hem of her dress, quickly pulling it up to her waist. She grew breathless as he dropped to his knees before her, spread her thighs wide and dipped his head in between her legs. Taking her clitoris into his mouth, he sucked furiously, sending needle sharp points of pleasure to her core.

He pushed two fingers inside her wet cunt. Sensations swamped her when he reached lower and touched her anus.

She never imagined his touch there would be so erotic. Taking one of his fingers, dripping with her juices, he carefully pushed it inside her back portal and tremors wracked her body as a powerful climax sent her racing off into total oblivion.

"Ah, you enjoyed that did you? I would love to slide my cock deep inside your pretty rosette. If you think my finger felt good, you'll love the feel of my prick."

Amelia was taken aback by this. Never in a million years would she have imagined something like that even possible. "Do people actually do something this depraved? I'm not sure I would enjoy it. You're so large, I would be afraid it might hurt."

"Oh, there's a way to ease my entry, and besides, a little pain can intensify your pleasure." Picking her up, he carried her through their dressing room and into his bedchamber. When they reached the bed, he tugged and tussled until he had removed her gown, all the while kissing her deeply. Once her clothes were off, leaving her naked, he told her, "Get on your hands and knees. I'll show you what pleasure there is to be found."

Amelia wasn't sure she wanted this, though a deeper part of her found the notion so wickedly tantalizing she did as he asked. Once she knelt in the center of his bed with her bottom raised waiting for what was to come, her heart beat a staccato and her legs trembled. She couldn't believe she was going to let him do this. Was she out of her mind? Her voice trembled as she asked, "You promise to stop, if I tell you to?"

"I promise. This will bring you pleasure beyond your wildest imagination." Warren opened the drawer of his bedside table and pulled out a bottle of liquid. "This oil will help open you up." He poured some on her derriere and rubbed it around her puckered entry. Electricity shot to her dripping wet core when he pushed a finger inside. She felt a slight sting, but it only heightened her desire. He had removed his breeches and as she glanced back over her shoulder, she watched as he stroked his manhood with more of the oil, and then he knelt behind her with one leg braced against the side of her bottom.

Warren covered her as he reached around and gently pinched her love bud, sending shock waves thundering through her body. The scent of almond filled the air as he worked more of the oil into her. He gently pushed on her shoulders. "Relax your arms and lay your head on the bed."

This movement had her bottom angled up ready for his possession. Her heart pounded when another finger joined his first, stretching her open for him. Chills raced through her veins as he stroked his fingers in and out of her tight hole, all while he continued stroking the center of her desire with his other hand. Fiery flames burst through her when another powerful climax had her spinning out of control. As she reached her peak, he removed his fingers and pushed his shaft inside her. It burned as he pushed through the ring of tight muscle. However, it was quickly replaced by pleasure rushing to the heart of her womanhood as he began to stroke in and out.

In and out, he stroked with sure, vigorous strokes, pumping ever faster, filling her dark passage with his engorged cock. The feeling was beyond anything she could have ever imagined. Shudders racked through her body as another wave of intense pleasure swept through her. Warren thrust one more time, and then he shouted out, "Oh, yes...that's it. It feels so fucking good. I love fucking your tight little ass. I'm...ah, yes, yes...I'm coming." He gasped for breath, and slumped over her as her shaking knees gave way, unable to hold her up any longer.

He nuzzled her neck. While the heaviness of his body pressed down on her, she still enjoyed the closeness. When he rolled off, she felt deprived, but only for a moment, because Warren pulled her back against him.

He murmured, "That was the most incredible sexual experience of my life. Thank you for giving me your trust. It's been a fantasy of mine for years. I think you thoroughly enjoyed it, possibly even more than I did. You climaxed several times."

Snuggling close against him, she breathed in and out as her heartbeat returned to a slower pace. "I never realized anything like that existed. I enjoyed it tremendously. I hope we can do it again, just not right away. I am a trifle sore and very sleepy."

"Lay here and rest for a while until you regain your strength."

Amelia closed her eyes and sleep swept her away.

Chapter 8

Damn!

Warren couldn't leave her alone. Never in his entire life had he experienced such pleasure. As he had pounded her ass, tidal waves of sublime passion swept through every part of his body. While he had fantasized about having anal sex for years, he'd never been with a partner he trusted enough. Her dark passage had hugged his cock like a silken glove. Thinking of their interlude had him fully aroused again. Of course, he couldn't give in to his desires, because she would be sore. Besides, he needed to return her to her room without waking her.

He slipped out of bed and went into the bathing chamber, cleaned himself, then went back to the bed. Careful not to waken her, he picked her up and carried her through their dressing rooms into her bedchamber. He laid her down and pulled the covers up, covering her luscious body. Amelia snuggled against her pillows and sighed, but didn't awaken.

When he entered his room, he gathered her clothes and put them in her dressing room. Afterward, he went back to the dressing room and dressed. Looking back on the afternoon, he realized he had enjoyed spending time with her and the children. He would need to make time to do that more often. With the youngsters around, he should be able to avoid a private conversation with her.

Of course they were married. He couldn't spend the rest of his life avoiding her. He found her intelligent and did enjoy talking to her. As long as he kept his heart closed, mayhap he should spend more time with her. After all, companionship was desirable in a marriage, and he certainly enjoyed the marriage bed.

Warren spent the rest of the afternoon going over reports Humphries left for him. It continued to rain and stayed cold. Even with a blazing fire in the hearth, shivers ran down his back. His fingers were tinged with blue and so cold he could barely hold a quill. Hearing the clock on the mantle chime six times, he went upstairs to dress for dinner. His valet met him at the door. "Your bath is prepared, and I laid out your bottle green redingote and gold waistcoat, my lord. Do you want your black pantaloons or the ivory ones?"

"The black, Hendricks. I shan't need you again this evening."

"Very good, sir. I shall return in the morning." After his valet left, Warren took his bath and dressed for the evening ahead. When he entered the drawing room, Aunt Bernice and Amelia were waiting for him. As soon as he showed up, Abercrombie announced dinner.

Conversation flowed freely around the dinner table. Amelia apparently looked forward to the ball the following evening.

While she discussed the event, Warren watched her. Her eyes sparkled with anticipation, and he decided to make sure she wasn't disappointed. Normally a young woman of twenty would have experienced two years of society. His new wife hadn't had that opportunity. It was only natural for her to be excited over her first ball.

Once they finished eating, Aunt Bernice suggested they go to the music room. She offered to play so Amelia could sing. His aunt knew the music to Amelia's favorite aria, and as she sang, he sat spellbound by the beauty of her clear, light soprano voice. When she told them the aria suited her voice she hadn't been exaggerating. She had the voice of an angel, and he could listen to her all night. By the time she ended the piece, moisture gathered in the corner of his eyes and a glow invaded his body from the sheer beauty of her final note.

Standing up, he walked over to her and touched her face. "My dear, your voice is magnificent. If you hadn't told me your stepmother taught you to sing, I would think you had studied under a great master."

Amelia blushed. "Thank you, I'm glad you enjoyed it. I would be happy to sing for you any time."

"You do have a remarkable voice," Aunt Bernice stated. "When the ton hears you, you will be in high demand at musicales."

"Oh, I couldn't sing in front of a whole room of people. Singing for family is one thing, performing for strangers, I would be terrified."

Wanting to put her at ease, Warren spoke up. "Don't worry. You shan't have to sing for anyone if you don't want to. It's just that you do have such an incredible talent, others would enjoy hearing you. I hope you'll sing for my mother again. She would love hearing you sing that aria."

"Of course, I will be happy to, but no strangers," she demurred with a shudder.

Stifling a yawn, Aunt Bernice stood. "My dear, I think I shall retire for the night. You may want to get a good night's sleep, because tomorrow will be a full day."

Amelia gave her a hug. "I took a long nap this afternoon, so I'm not tired. I think I will select a book to read. See you in the morning." Aunt Bernice kissed her cheek and left the room.

"Let me escort you to the library. I need to go to my study. I have some reports I need to go over tonight. As you know, we are taking the final vote on the bill tomorrow afternoon. I want to be prepared." Warren offered her his arm and walked her to the library, and with a bow, he went down the hall to his study.

He worked for several hours on reports, and when the clock struck midnight, he went upstairs. When he reached the landing, he looked to the left and saw light coming from beneath Amelia's bedchamber door. Could she have fallen asleep reading? Worrying that the lamp might cause a fire, he went over to her door and lightly tapped. Not hearing a response, he turned the knob and peeked in the room. Just what he suspected, she had fallen asleep, the book open against her chest, and the lamp burning on the bedside table.

Quietly, he moved over to the bed, picked up the book and laid it on the table, bending over he placed a soft kiss on her forehead. Her gorgeous auburn curls were all tousled around her head, and his breath caught at the sheer beauty of the sight. He felt a crack in the shield he had built around his heart. If he didn't feel it would betray Lucinda's memory, he could grow to love Amelia. After turning down the lamp, he made his way back to his room, feeling the weight of guilt pressing down on his shoulders.

After Warren crawled into bed, it took him a long time to fall asleep. Thoughts of Lucinda raced through his mind. Feelings for Amelia clashed with his love for his late wife. He tossed and turned for hours, battling the growing feelings for his new wife and his sense of betrayal for having them. Eventually, he gave up on sleep and rose from the bed. He went across the room to the table and poured himself a large glass of brandy, drinking it down in a few gulps. He went over to the dresser and picked up the miniature of Lucinda and hugged it to his heart.

Oh, God, why?

If you hadn't taken her from me, I wouldn't be in this torment.

His heart raced a mile a minute as he tried to imagine Lucinda's gentle touch. All he could feel was the silken skin of his new wife. He grabbed the bottle of brandy and flung himself into the chair in front of the fire. Warren finished off the bottle, becoming quite foxed before he finally fell into a troubled sleep.

Amelia awoke the next morning, with sunlight streaming through her window. Glancing over at the clock on the mantle, she noticed the time. A tap at the door heralded the arrival of her new lady's maid. Sophie had helped her find Ella, and she had worked out well so far. She certainly could do marvelous things with her hair. Of course, she would have rather kept Susan. Sophie had told her she needed someone who understood how to dress a countess and while Susan was sweet, she didn't have the proper training.

Ella entered the room carrying her breakfast tray. Amelia's stomach growled and she tucked into her breakfast. After she finished eating, she stepped onto her balcony and the change in the weather astonished her. The sun shone brightly. It was a gorgeous warm spring day. Such was the weather in England in the spring, one day dreary and cold and the next warm and sunny.

Stepping back inside her room, she glanced at the ormolu clock. She should have enough time to see the children. They were doing math when she arrived, and she listened to her brother and sister while they gave the answers to the problems the governess had them working on. Their ability to do the math surprised her. Of course, she had always been aware they were bright children. Miss Hilton allowed the children a short break from their studies and they gathered around Amelia, wanting her to tell them a story. Since Lawrence hadn't heard the tale of King Arthur, she shared that one with him.

When she finished, Lawrence clapped his hands. "What a great story. I want to be a knight when I grow up. I will protect all the damsels in distress from the dragons. Can we go back to the park today, Mama?"

Amelia's heart melted every time he called her by that endearment. He was such an adorable little boy, and it pleased her immensely that he had accepted her so readily. Evidently, he missed a mother's love. "We can go if you finish your studies by two. Your grandmother is holding a ball this evening to celebrate my marriage to your father. It must be a short trip."

"Oh, goody. Do you think we will have time to fly our kites?" Lawrence asked.

Justin and Carrie chimed in, "Please?"

Amelia smiled. "I think that can be arranged. If we are going to fly kites, you need to return to your studies. I'll come back and get you at two." After giving all three children hugs, she left for her meeting with the housekeeper.

Since Aunt Bernice had agreed to help her learn household management, she had already arrived in Mrs. Goodall's office. They spent a couple of hours discussing various housekeeping issues, and Amelia didn't find household management difficult at all. She actually found it quite enjoyable, although, this wasn't as big of a household as she would find at Broadmoor Manor. Here there were just ten servants, including her maid.

After their meeting with the housekeeper, they met with Chef Philippe and planned all the menus through Friday morning when they were due to leave for Essex. From what Warren told her, Broadmoor Manor was five miles north of Chelmsford, the closest town to his estate, making it around thirty-five miles from London. While she would miss Aunt Bernice and Sophie, she looked forward to seeing her new home. They had been very welcoming to her and seemed pleased over their marriage. Although, if they ever found out how they really met, they wouldn't be as welcoming. She pushed that horrifying thought from her mind, relieved that the two of them were the only ones who knew, and neither she nor Warren would tell a soul.

Amelia picked the children up with their kites in hand and went across the street to Grosvenor Square. Thank goodness the weather had warmed back up from yesterday. Lawrence and her brother and sister would have great weather to fly their kites, what with the warm spring breeze blowing. She inhaled and the fragrant scent of the lovely blooms throughout the park filled her senses. Spring was always her favorite season.

Looking for a nice open area for the kites, she spied a good spot and led the children to it. Once she helped them launch their kites in the air, she sat down on the park bench, slightly out of breath from her exertion. Living in London had her out of shape. That would be another benefit of living in the country again. She needed to get more exercise. Long walks and riding a horse again would accomplish that. It was so thoughtful of him to give her Genevieve. She couldn't wait to ride her.

Looking back on what happened yesterday afternoon, Amelia felt her womanly flesh ache with need. What they did yesterday was so wicked, but oh, so pleasurable. The thought of him taking her that way had her dripping wet to the point she squirmed in her seat. She never imagined she could be so wanton. The marriage bed was much more exciting than she ever expected. It wasn't just the marriage bed she found so enjoyable. What time she had spent with her husband showed her how intelligent and kind he was. The man had even suggested the dolls for Carrie. How exceptional. She greatly feared she was losing her heart to her husband.

At least she had made some progress yesterday. They actually had some conversation before they let their passions take over. Now, if she could just get him to continue talking to her. The children were the answer. One thing Amelia was confident of, Warren loved his son and would never turn down any plans involving him.

Suddenly a strong gust of wind whipped Carrie's kite from her hands and blew it into a tree. Carrie burst into tears, and Amelia ran to her. "I'm sorry, darling. We'll go find one of the footmen and see if he can retrieve your kite. Lawrence, Justin, reel your kites in. It's time for us to go back inside."

Once the boys had their kites down, they trooped back across the street. One of the footmen opened the door to let them in, and Amelia sent him over to retrieve her sister's kite. He returned in a few minutes with a slightly damaged one. With a few minor repairs, it should be good as new, ready for the next outing. She took the children upstairs to the schoolroom, and turned them over to the nursemaid, after giving the youngsters hugs and kisses.

Amelia spent the rest of the afternoon getting ready for the ball. When Ella finished doing her hair, she stood before the mirror and astonishment showed on her face. Her eyes took in the deep cream ball gown with Belgian lace covering the bodice and flounced around the hem. She looked so elegant and sophisticated. Her blood tingled in her veins, at the thought of going to her first ball.

The only problem she saw with her appearance was her bare neck. She needed something to accent the gown, but since she didn't own any jewels she would have to make do. There was a tap at the dressing room door, and Warren entered in all his evening finery. Her eyes traveled down, taking in his trim hips and muscular thighs, encased in cream-colored evening knee breeches. White stockings clung to his well-defined calves. He looked so appealing she immediately felt a fierce wave of pleasure rush to her nether region.

Coming over to her, he placed a kiss on the center of her palm, sending chills up her arm. "My dear, you look ravishing. I brought you some jewels for tonight. I figured you would need something. This emerald necklace has been in the family for generations."

Opening a red velvet box, she gasped. "Oh, my lord, it's beautiful. I just told my maid I needed a necklace with this gown."

"Turn around, and I'll put it on you." The warm brush of fingers on the nape of her neck as he fastened the necklace sent tingles rushing to her womb. The slightest touch had her tactile senses going wild. Warren turned her around and smiled with appreciation glowing in his eyes. "Ah, yes, perfect."

"Thank you. I promise I shan't lose it."

Reaching into his pocket, he removed another small velvet box. "Here is something else. I bought them for you when I purchased your ring. They should go well with the necklace. I hope you like them."

Overwhelmed, Amelia's hands trembled as she accepted the box. Nestled inside, was a pair of stunning emerald earbobs circled with diamonds. "They're gorgeous. Will you put them on me?" As he slipped them in her ears, icy fingers of awareness shot through her. Then he gently kissed the right side of her neck, sending desire racing to her feminine core.

Once the earbobs were on, Amelia looked in the mirror. "I look like a princess from one of the fairy tales I read to the children."

"You're beautiful. I'll be the envy of all the men tonight with you on my arm. Shall we go downstairs and join Aunt Bernice?"

Taking his offered arm, Warren escorted her downstairs to the drawing room, where they joined Aunt Bernice. Shortly after they arrived, Abercrombie told them dinner was served. Amelia was pleased with her menu choices. She preened when Warren made several comments regarding his enjoyment of the food.

After they finished dining, Warren escorted the ladies to the carriage. On the way to the ball, Amelia found herself tapping her foot. She couldn't wait to arrive and see all the other women in their beautiful, colorful evening gowns, dancing under hundreds of candles in great chandeliers.

Once the carriage came to a stop, a footman in splendid livery came forward and lowered the steps. Warren exited and then, turning back, offered his assistance to Amelia and Aunt Bernice. A red carpet ran the length of the pavement, placed there to protect their evening slippers. Now, she truly felt like a princess. She accepted Warren's arm and they made their way up the steps and entered the foyer, where they found Sophie and Clayton waiting for them.

Sophie gave Amelia a warm welcome and a hug. "Darling, you look stunning." With a twinkle in her eyes, she told her son, "You will need to watch her closely tonight or another gentleman may very well steal her away."

"Never fear, Mother, I shall stay by her side all evening. That way I can fight off her many admirers."

All this talk made her nervous. While it pleased her that they both thought she looked nice, she certainly didn't want strange men fawning all over her. After all, she was a married woman, not a young debutant. It reassured her that her husband planned to stay by her side.

Amelia glanced around the ballroom at the beautifully decorated room with its large vases of hot house roses and lilies, and her senses came alive from the various scents wafting through the room. A short time later, the other guests began to arrive and for the next hour, Amelia greeted one lord and lady after another, so many that her head was spinning. There was no way she would remember any of their names. At last, they dissolved the receiving line and went into the ball room to start the dancing.

Warren led her onto the dance floor as the opening strains of a waltz filled the room. Placing his arm around her waist and clasping her hand, he swept her around the dance floor for her first dance at a London ball. Shivers of excitement raced through her veins as she glanced at all the other couples joining them.

He smiled down at her. "So, what do you think? Is it everything you expected?"

"It's more than I ever imagined. It's so nice of your mother to do this for us. She's gone to a great deal of effort to make sure tonight is special."

"My mother enjoys entertaining, so this was diverting for her. We will be presented to everyone right before the supper dance. I want you to relax and enjoy yourself this evening."

"Oh, I plan to. Dancing the waltz with someone other than my father is quite invigorating. You dance divinely, and I feel as if I'm floating on air."

He gave her a smoldering look with his golden eyes. "I would rather have you in my arms in bed than on a dance floor."

Laughing up at him, she whispered, "Be quiet, my lord. Someone might hear you," then changing the subject, she asked, "How did the vote go this afternoon?"

"Thank God, we defeated the bill. The Duke of Rutland made all the difference in the world. Without his support the bill would have passed, and our nation would have gone through some tough economic times. Mallory is out celebrating the victory. That's why he's not here. His idea of celebrating doesn't include attending a ball."

"I can imagine what his idea of entertainment means, and I'm sure a woman is part of it."

He laughed. "Of course, my dear, you're correct. Ah, our dance has ended. Shall we join my mother and Clayton?"

They made their way across the dance floor and found Sophie and Clayton by the refreshments table. The rest of the evening flew by. They danced practically every dance. Everyone was polite and courteous, and she felt welcomed and accepted by the ton. It fulfilled every one of her girlhood dreams.

Her husband remained extraordinarily attentive throughout the evening and never left her side. The delicacies at supper were superb, and Warren had her laughing over some amusing tales of his antics with Mallory while they grew up. It felt good to see him laughing, since he was normally so serious most of the time. She hoped this meant he was beginning to enjoy spending time with her, and not just in bed.

By the time they made it back home, Amelia barely kept her eyes open long enough to disrobe and make it to bed. She fell asleep before her head hit the pillow. Her dreams were filled with visions of all the titillating things she experienced that night. She had truly been — the belle of the ball.

Chapter 9

The next four days flew by. The countess had them attending a different entertainment each evening. One afternoon, they even went to a garden party in Richmond at the estate of one of Warren's peers. Since they stayed out so late each night, Amelia slept well into the morning the next day. Once she arose, Sophie took her on morning calls throughout the afternoon. The few times she had seen the children; they appeared happy and had adjusted well to their new situation. While her brother and sister may not be missing her, she certainly missed them. She saw very little of Warren during the day, and by the time they made it home each night, she fell asleep once her head touched her pillow. They hadn't made love in several days.

Her plan to spend more time with her husband wasn't working very well. At the musicale they had attended, his attention wandered. On the evenings when they attended a ball, he danced one waltz with her and then went to the card room where he spent the rest of the night, leaving her with his mother and aunt. While Amelia enjoyed their company, she would have rather spent time with Warren.

The sun shone brightly on Friday morning, and the weather was unseasonably warm for May. From what Warren had told her, it should only take five hours to reach Broadmoor Manor, so the children and Miss Hilton rode with her. The luggage carriage wouldn't hold them, plus Ella, Hendricks and Abercrombie. Her husband rode his horse, Devil, since there would not be any more room inside for him.

Around noon, Warren broke the trip, so they could enjoy luncheon at a coaching inn along the way. After they finished their meal, Amelia suggested, "Why don't we let the children run and play by the pond a few minutes? Being closed up in the carriage for hours is hard on them. They've actually been well behaved and deserve a treat."

He glanced at her over the table. "I suppose it wouldn't hurt to let them play for a little while. We're making good time and should arrive by three."

"Thank you. I know the children will be pleased."

After helping her arise from the chair, Warren led her from the private dining room. They joined Miss Hilton and her charges outside and Amelia told the children they could play. She watched them run over to the pond, and Lawrence began showing Justin and Carrie how to skip rocks.

Warren offered her his arm. "I know my mother kept you busy. We attended an entertainment each evening, and then she took you on morning calls the next day. I hope she didn't run you too ragged."

"I have been busy to say the least. If this is a taste of what a London season is like, I don't know how everyone keeps it up.

I'm exhausted after five days. I can't imagine doing it for months on end."

He patted her hand, in a reassuring manner. "You shall have no worries regarding that, my dear. I detest the season. If it weren't for my obligations to the lords, I doubt I would ever go back. After working on this last bill, I know I can no longer shirk my responsibilities. Although we will be in London, it doesn't mean we need to attend parties every evening. Now that you've been introduced to the *ton*, we can pick and choose what entertainments we want to attend."

"Thank goodness. That's wonderful news. I did enjoy attending the opera, though. And I would love to attend the theater. However, going to a party every night is too much. I haven't spent any time with the children. Monday afternoon was the last time I did anything with them other than a few minutes here and there. No wonder most children of the *ton* spend very little time with their parents. I'm not used to that. I don't believe it's good for the children."

"I agree completely. While my father spent time in London when the lords sat, and my mother went for the season, they brought me along. No matter how busy they were, they always made time for me."

"Speaking of the lords, will we be returning to London soon?"

"I must return in two weeks. There's another vote coming up, and I have to be there." He removed his pocket watch and looked at the time. "We need to gather the children. It's time to resume our journey if we're going to make it home in time for tea."

The rest of the trip remained uneventful, and they reached Broadmoor Manor by three. The servant's coach hadn't stopped for luncheon, so it arrived well before them. Abercrombie had all the servants lined up to meet their new mistress. While a bit overwhelming for her, Amelia hid it well and smiled at each servant, repeating their names back to them. That always helped her remember people better.

The housekeeper, Mrs. Wyatt, offered to show her the rooms she would occupy. Warren declined. "I shall show my wife our suite. Please make sure tea is ready when we return."

Miss Hilton herded the children upstairs. Warren took Amelia's arm and guided her upstairs. He showed her into a beautifully appointed sitting room, decorated in various shades of blue with a touch of gold. The highly polished floor gleamed around the Aubusson carpet. A marble hearth filled the far wall and a lovely gold brocade sofa sat in front of it with Hepplewhite tables on each end. French doors led onto a balcony. She would have liked to go outside and look around, but Warren led her to a door across the room.

"This will be your bedchamber." Opening the door, he stepped back, allowing her to enter first. "The arrangement of our suite is similar to our London townhouse. The bedchambers have dressing rooms separating them. You'll also have your own private bath. These rooms were restored recently." He smiled over at her. "However, I'm sure they could benefit from a fair lady's touch. This is the part of the house damaged by the fire."

"I would never have known. You did an excellent job repairing the damage, and the rooms are perfect the way they are. I shan't change a thing. Can I see your rooms?"

"Certainly, my dear." Warren led her through her spacious dressing room and through his, and then they entered his bedchamber. It was also done in blue with a masculine flare.

An enormous bed stood on a raised dais with deep blue velvet bed curtains and a matching counterpane. Amelia's body tensed as images of them making love in that bed flooded her mind. She glanced over at him and saw the depth of his eyes deepen to molten amber.

He pulled her close and gave her a passionate kiss, driving his tongue in the deep cavity of her mouth. Amelia responded with equal fervor. Sweeping her up, he carried her over to the bed and dropped her in the middle of it, falling on top of her while he continued to devour her mouth.

Warren pushed her gown up to her waist, ripped open his trousers, pushed his smalls out of the way and surged home, driving deep into her dripping wet core. His tongue stroked her teeth and mouth as he mirrored each one of his thrusts into her tight sheath. She wrapped her arms around his neck, digging in her nails while the tension built, winding tighter and tighter. Her passion spiraled higher and higher. Amelia's inner muscles clenched around his shaft. She went soaring ever higher until she flew over the cliff, and then Warren shouted out his own release. His body went limp as he slumped on top of her. She clasped him to her, luxuriating in the feel of his body close against hers, his ragged breathing music to her ears. If they could feel such explosive passion for each other, surely it was more than lust.

"I'm sorry," he murmured. "My weight must be crushing you. You've made me weak, sweetheart. I can't get enough of you."

Rolling to the side, he pulled her close, and she nestled her head in the crook of his shoulder. While she breathed in the scent of clean, male sweat, her heartbeat returned to normal.

"I'm yours whenever you want me. I can't get enough of you either. I never imagined I could be such a wanton."

With a teasing tone, he pointed out, "Wanton is good, just make sure you reserve it for your husband."

Glancing up at him, she seductively rejoined, "As long as you're just wicked with me, I shall only be a wanton with you. I'm sure you can keep me well satisfied."

"Never fear, my dear, I shall keep you so satisfied you shan't have the energy to contemplate another. All teasing aside, while we met in such an unorthodox manner, I know you will always be faithful, and I shall be to you. I realize you are fiercely loyal."

She hesitated, not wanting to make him angry but then decided to tell him what she thought. It wasn't in her nature to avoid confrontation. She had to speak her mind. "Warren…I truly don't expect your love, though I do want your friendship. I know you stay away from my bed because you don't want to fall in love with me. Please don't. I miss it terribly when you don't come to me. You've ignited my passion, and I burn for you every day."

He turned her face toward him and tenderly touched her lips. "I suppose it will be safe, as long as you understand I can never offer you my love. I promise I shan't avoid you any longer. After all, we'll be married for the rest of our lives, and I don't want dissension between us. Now, I'm sure our tea will be cold if we don't hurry. Why don't you return to your chamber and freshen up? When I meet you downstairs at four, I will give you a guided tour."

With a smile on her face, Amelia rose from the bed, gave him a quick kiss on the cheek, and hurried from the room. Once back in her chamber, she hugged herself. Warren agreed he would quit avoiding her. When he had kissed her without any sexual intent, fierce waves of tenderness had rushed through her. Whether he realized it or not, he was ready to throw off the bindings holding him to his past, and she was just the person to help him do it.

Warren watched his wife leave his room. He had no regrets over promising that he would spend more time with her. After all, they were married, and it would make the marriage unbearable if he constantly tried to avoid her. She had proven she was a good mother for Lawrence, and he wanted that for his son. He also wanted more children and wanted them with Amelia.

All he needed to do was keep the brick wall around his heart intact. He stood up, walked over and picked up the miniature of Lucinda on the dresser. Sighing deeply, he stroked the image of her beloved face. Amelia and Mallory were right—it was time for him to rejoin the living.

But how can I do this and still honor Lucinda's memory? Would it betray her if I open myself up to friendship with my new wife?

Lucinda would want him to experience joy in his life. Something told him he could find happiness with Amelia. He took the picture, opened the top dresser drawer and gently laid it face down. He would give their marriage a chance, and not just in the marriage bed. He'd spend time with Amelia every day, so he could learn more about her. With determination in his step, he went downstairs to join her.

He started his new campaign at tea. When she entered the drawing room, he greeted her with a smile and kissed her cheek. "You look lovely, my dear. I think our tea is still hot. Please take a seat and pour me a cup."

"I will be happy to."

Her cheeks grew flushed and hope glowed in the green depths of her eyes. His softer approach must have pleased her. A sense of rightness settled in his chest. Perhaps, he could show Amelia affection and caring without betraying Lucinda.

She prepared the tea and also handed him a plate of sandwiches with one of the cook's special lemon cakes. He accepted the plate. "Try one of these tortes. They are one of Mrs. Jarvis's specialties. She makes them whenever I'm in residence. She knows I love them."

Amelia added a torte to her plate. "I suppose I could try one. I do love anything lemon. I checked on the children. Justin and Carrie seem to like their new rooms, and they are fascinated by all the toys in the nursery. Thank you for thinking of Carrie. She loves the dollhouse and the tea table and chairs. She had it set with her new tea set and all her dolls. Justin also enjoyed the toys Lawrence showed him. It pleases me greatly that the children are getting along well."

"I'm thankful my son finally has some companions his own age. Lawrence rarely has other children his age to play with as the village is too far from my estate."

They continued discussing the children while they finished their tea. Warren enjoyed watching Amelia. She grew quite animated when she talked, especially when the subject concerned the children. Anyone who heard her would know how much she loved her siblings, and she now included his son in that circle of love. It relieved his mind greatly that his son had taken so well to Amelia. They also discussed his estate, and she asked some thought provoking questions. He wasn't surprised. He had ascertained her high level of intelligence over the last ten days.

Looking down at their empty plates, he arose from the sofa. "Since we've devoured our tea, my dear, let me show you the rest of the house."

Warren gave her some history as he gave her the tour. While strolling through the portrait gallery, he pointed out all his ancestors, telling Amelia several amusing stories about his notorious kin, especially his grandfather who had been a courtier at King George III's court during the conflict with America.

"One of my great-uncles migrated to America as a young man back in 1750. He turned his coat, when the fighting broke out for independence. From his line, I have several distant cousins who live in a place called Williamsburg, Virginia." He went on to explain, "Through the years, I have corresponded with them, and I want to go visit them at some point. Of course, they live on a large plantation with hundreds of slaves, and I've strongly opposed slavery my entire time in the House of Lords. However, I do think it would be fascinating to see how they live."

"I think it would be interesting too. I would love to visit America. My father showed me a copy of their Declaration of Independence. Have you ever read it? It's quite remarkable actually. I think it would be wonderful to live in a country with that much freedom. They believe *all* men are created equal and deserve the same rights, whether they're a servant or a landowner. My father admired the industrious Americans greatly and considered emigrating there as a young man. My mother wouldn't hear of it. She feared all the stories she had heard regarding the Indians."

Reaching over, he gently touched her arm. "That is fortunate for me. If your father had moved there, we would never have met. I think...that would have been a terrible loss. Amelia, I want to give our marriage a chance. I avoided you when we were in town, but no more. I want us to have an amicable marriage." By this time, they were back at the staircase. "As pleasant as this has been, I have a meeting with my steward, Mr. Monroe. I look forward to seeing you at dinner." He laughed lightening the mood. "You might want to rest because I have prodigious plans for you tonight, my lady."

"Good. I'm pleased that you do. I think a nap would be sensible. I'm counting on *you* to keep me awake." Casting him an alluring smile, she headed upstairs.

He watched her swaying ass as she made her way up the stairs. Thinking of the night to come had him hard as a rock. He could feel his raging cock sliding into her cunt, or possibly her ass again. Before he did that though, he would nibble on her succulent clitoris. These thoughts weren't going to help him in his meeting, so getting control of himself, he went to his study.

Warren had a productive meeting with Monroe. All the planting had gone well, and several of his cows had given birth to healthy offspring. If the weather were to cooperate this coming summer, he would be set for another abundant harvest in the fall.

After dinner that night, neither one of them was in the mood to read, so they went upstairs to their rooms. When they arrived outside her door, he stroked her cheek. "I'll give you fifteen minutes, then I shall come to you. Be ready for me."

Amelia gave him a coy look. "As you wish, my lord. I shall be waiting for you." Reaching up, she gave him a playful kiss, and then went through the door before he had a chance to respond.

He entered his room and dismissed Hendricks as was a usual habit. He didn't even let his valet see him unclothed. Hurrying through his nightly regime, he pulled on a nightshirt and silently cursed. He wanted to feel her soft skin, to have their bodies touch, but he couldn't let her see him. Perhaps if he blew out all the candles he could risk removing the nightshirt. Yes, that's what he would do. After tying the dressing gown around his waist, he went to her room.

When he entered, Amelia sat at her dressing table brushing her hair. She looked over at him and smiled. Warren approached her and took the brush from her hand. "Allow me." He ran the brush through her silken tresses. Stroke after stroke, he brushed her hair until it shone. Pushing it to the side, he leaned down and kissed the nape of her neck. Reaching around her, he touched her breast through her sheer night rail, and her nipple grew taut. "Ah, so responsive."

He laid the brush down and pulled her up into his arms, toppling over the dressing stool in a rush to hold her. He carried her to the bed, and laid her down on the silken sheets. "I'll put out the lights." He went around the room blowing out all the candles and turning down the lamp. With the drapes closed, the room was completely dark. He took off his robe, pulled the nightshirt off over his head and laid it at the foot of the bed, then crawled in with her. He went to pull her close. It was so dark, he couldn't find her. This wasn't going to work. He couldn't see a damned thing. Hell, he couldn't even find her mouth to kiss her.

"God's teeth!" he muttered.

"What's wrong?"

"I shall return in a moment." Getting out of bed, he reached for the nightshirt and pulled it back on. He fumbled around until he got the lamp lit again. "Amelia, I must blindfold you tonight. I want to feel your skin against mine. If you promise you will not touch my chest, I shan't tie you up. Will you do this for me?"

She looked over at him, but disappointment shone in her eyes even though she nodded her ascent. Searching the pocket of his dressing gown, he located a silk handkerchief, tied it around her eyes and climbed back in bed, after he took off the nightshirt. "I want to see your gorgeous naked body. Take off your night rail."

Amelia pulled it off and lay back down on the bed. Warren gazed upon her and felt his cock harden to painful proportions, and yet his tormented mind sensed her disappointment. He gathered her close. "I'm sorry, my dear. I can't let you see me. I'm not ready yet. Once the doctor told me I was healed, I took a look. The scars were red and ugly, grotesque, beyond anything I had ever imagined. Since then, I haven't allowed anyone to see me naked, not even my valet. I can't bear to look at my body in a mirror without clothes on. It's all I can do to make myself wash thoroughly each day. I either keep my eyes closed or look at the ceiling while I bathe."

Amelia gasped as she looked at him. "Are you telling me you haven't looked at your scars in three years? Oh, Warren, that's just too sad. Do you realize they may not be that bad? Burns are red and angry looking at first. However, scars do fade over time. My stepmother burned her forearm badly, and it looked horrible for months. By the time the scarring faded, the burn was hardly noticeable."

He stiffened and sat up, releasing her. "Dammit. Amelia. I'm sure her burn wasn't as severe as mine!" He stood and jerked on his dressing gown. "I can't do this." He threw her what had to be a scathing look. "I don't want to talk about this anymore. You cannot begin to understand what it's like for me. I'm hideous. I will not let you or anyone else see me. I'm going to my room." He stalked over to the dressing room door, flung it open, and blasted through it, slamming the door behind him.

Chapter 10

Amelia tore off the blindfold, as Warren stomped from the room. She lay there stunned over what had happened. She was aware of his sensitivity regarding his scars, but she didn't mean to make him angry. Though…was it really anger? Mayhap—it was pain instead and he just acted angry. How sad. Warren couldn't bear to look at his own body. Oh, Lord, why couldn't she learn to keep her mouth shut?

When she looked back on his reaction, she suspected that he was tormented over more than just the scars. Today, he had let his guard down and allowed them a chance to get closer, to begin building a caring relationship. Her heart ached for him. All she wanted to do was pull him close and take his pain away, but he wasn't going to give her that chance. This could negate the progress she had made over the last couple of days. Now, he would probably avoid her like the plague.

She turned down the lamp and snuggled up with the pillow where he had lain. His masculine scent clung to it, and she silently wept. It was no longer friendship she wanted from him. She wanted — no she needed — his love. She was in love with her husband.

After tossing and turning for what seemed like hours, she fell into a restless sleep. When she awoke the next morning, her eyes ached and her head hurt, so she had her maid bring her a cold compress. When Ella returned with the cloth, Amelia sent her away, telling her she wasn't ready to arise yet.

As she lay there, hoping her headache would ease, she pondered what had happened the night before. It would be best if she pretended it never happened. She would be cheerful and playful with him, hoping he would get over last night's debacle. Now that they had arrived at the manor, she would persuade him to take her riding. Perhaps they would come across a secluded spot and she could seduce him.

Ringing for her maid, she rushed through her toilette and dressed in her new riding habit. She hurried from her room, so she could catch her husband before he left. When she entered the breakfast room, he sat at the table, reading the newspaper. She approached the sideboard, filled her plate and joined him. "Good morning. Isn't it a lovely day? I hope you will take me riding around the estate this morning. I'm so excited over meeting Genevieve. Please say you'll take me?" She glanced over at him, giving him a bright smile.

He laid the paper down, and met her gaze. "I suppose we could do that. I'll go to the stables and have the grooms saddle our horses. By the time you've finished eating, our mounts should be ready." He stood up, gave her a bow and left the breakfast room.

Amelia hurried through her morning meal, then hastened to the stables. When she arrived, Warren stood by a gorgeous chestnut mare. Her hands itched to hold the reins in her palms again. It had been almost a year since she had last ridden, and she wanted to feel Genevieve under her command. Reaching her hand up, she stroked the mare's nose. "Good morning, my beauty. I have a feeling we're going to become good friends." Turning toward Warren, she said, "Thank you for Genevieve, my lord. She's beautiful."

"I thought you would like her. Here let me help you and we shall be off. I thought I would show you the home farm today. Then, I will take you to meet my tenants another time."

Cupping his hands together for her, Amelia put her foot in them and mounted Genevieve. Once securely in the sidesaddle, she looked down and smiled. "This has been the longest eight months of my live. It feels marvelous being on a horse again and just think — she's mine. Come on, let's be off."

Warren mounted Devil and led the way out of the stable yard, and soon they were cantering along the path. They rode beside each other in companionable silence. Amelia longed to feel the cool, spring breeze caress her face, to ride as fast as the wind. This gentle trotting would never do. "Can we take them for a gallop?" She pointed toward an open field. "That field over there looks safe enough."

"You're correct. See that tree on the other side? I'll race you to it."

"You're on!" Then she dug her heels in and took off. As they raced along, the wind almost blew her hat off. Fortunately, the ribbons kept her from losing it completely. They were neck and neck, at the last minute, Warren pulled ahead as they reached the tree. Amelia laughed. "Well, at least I gave you a good run. That was exhilarating."

"You *are* a good rider. I had to push Devil to win. Follow me. I want to show you the lake. It's not too far from here."

They took off down the wooded path and soon they entered a clearing near a small lake. Warren helped her dismount, so they could stroll along the grassy bank. He offered her an arm, and she slid her hand through the crook. She sighed as she gazed around. "This is a beautiful spot. I'm sure you spent a great deal of time here while you were growing up. Lord Hollingsworth had a lake, and Bernard and I would sneak away and go fishing in the summer. Do you fish?"

"Oh, definitely. Mallory and I used to fish here every summer. I plan to teach Lawrence this year. Now, we can teach both boys. Do you think Carrie will want to learn?"

"Oh, I'm sure she will," she answered, letting excitement color her voice. "You know what would be nice? We can bring the children on a picnic, and after we eat, teach them to fish. Can we do it tomorrow?"

"I don't see why we couldn't. I need to spend some time with Monroe in the morning, but I can break free for the afternoon."

Stroking his arm in a playful way, Amelia gave him what she hoped was a come hither smile. "That sounds delightful. Uh, Warren, it seems private here. I wouldn't mind a kiss." If she could entice him into kissing her his passion would ignite, and hopefully he would make love to her.

His eyes darkened to a deep gold and desire flamed in their depths. He pulled her close and his lips swooped down on hers. Pinpricks raced across her skin and a heavy weight settled in her womb as she immersed herself in his embrace. He groaned as he pulled her closer and deepened their passionate kiss.

Reaching up, he slipped a hand under her jacket and kneaded her breast through the fabric of her blouse. Decadent pleasure thrummed through every muscle, rushing heat to her womanhood.

Amelia reached down and stroked him through his breeches. She felt his manhood swell under her hand. Warren pulled her down onto the soft grass along the bank of the lake. He pulled up her skirts and stroked her pussy. Moist heat gathered in her nether regions. "Ah, Amelia, I need to taste you." Moving down her body, he buried his head between her thighs and sucked her clitoris in his mouth. Pleasure raced up her spine as he laved her swollen flesh.

She let out a high keening scream as waves of molten lava poured through her veins and her release washed over her. Warren crawled up her body and gave her a searing kiss. Amelia wanted to give him his share of pleasure. Instinct took over, and she pushed him onto his back, ripped open his breeches and pulled his stiff erection out of his drawers. Unable to resist experiencing the feel of him between her lips, she wrapped her tongue around his manhood, sucking him deeply into the recesses of her mouth. She reveled in the taste and the earthy smell of arousal.

Warren moved his hips, stroking his shaft in and out of her mouth, sending it so deep it touched the back of her throat. She concentrated on relaxing her muscles so she could take all of him. Molding her lips tightly around his huge erection, she sucked strongly as he continued driving his cock in and out. Her pussy clinched in time with each thrust. It amazed her that she felt such strong desire, and he wasn't even touching her.

"I'm undone!" His release jetted out of him with surprising force. Amelia drank his essence as if it were nectar of the gods, relishing the warm salty taste of him. Warren's eyes rolled back in his head, as with a slight pop, his cock slipped from her lips. He reached down and pulled her up against his chest. "Thank you, I never dreamed you'd be willing to do this for me."

Amelia smugly looked up at him, feeling immensely pleased with herself. "So...you enjoyed that? I thought you would. I wanted to give you the same kind of pleasure you gave me."

"It was pleasure beyond anything I've felt before." She lay in his arms as he softly stroked her back for several minutes, enjoying the closeness of their bodies. Warren stirred. "While this has been immensely pleasurable, we need to put our clothing to rights. I don't think anyone will come along, but we *are* out in the open. When I'm with you, I lose all my senses."

"I love it when you lose control."

"Be that as it may, we need to be on our way if I'm going to show you the rest of the home farm." Warren stood and offered her his hand. With a smile on her face and joy in her heart, she placed her hand in his and let him pull her up. After helping her re-mount, they were on their way.

Warren was solicitous of her all morning and joined her for luncheon when they returned from the tour of the home farm. It relieved her mind, because even after last night's disaster, he still kept his word about spending time with her so they could get to know each other better.

That afternoon, Amelia joined the children and took them for a walk through the woods. The youngsters had a marvelous time playing hide-and-seek. There were dozens of tall oaks and a great many bushes they could hide behind. Her brother burrowed his way into a fallen tree to hide from his sister and new friend, but quickly scrambled back out when he discovered a black snake inside. It did her heart good to see how happy all three children were. Lawrence appeared to be in his element, showing Justin and Carrie all his favorite spots.

When they returned from their walk, Lawrence looked flushed and complained of a headache. Amelia noticed his nose was running and he had coughed several times.

Lawrence choked out in a scratchy voice, "I don't feel very well. My tummy hurts too." Once the words left his mouth, he doubled over and cast up his accounts. He fell on the ground as his eyes rolled back in his head.

Amelia swept him up and raced toward the house. She called back to Justin and Carrie, "Children follow me." Rushing into the house, she saw Abercrombie. "Call for a doctor. My stepson is ill. He's burning up with fever."

Before she started up the stairs, Warren came out of his study and when he saw his son lying limply in her arms, he rushed forward. "What's wrong with Lawrence?"

"I'm not sure, but he's quite ill. He complained of a headache and told me his stomach hurt. After throwing up, he passed out."

Warren barked at Abercrombie, "Don't just stand there. Send for the doctor posthaste."

"Certainly, my lord." The butler turned and hurried down the hall.

He reached for his son. "Here, let me carry him. He's too heavy for you." After taking Lawrence from her, he rushed upstairs with Amelia and the children following right behind him.

Carrie asked, "Is Lawrence going to be all right?"

When they made it to the top of the stairs, Amelia knelt and drew her brother and sister to her. "I'm sure he will be fine, but until we know what's wrong with Lawrence, I don't want you around him. Now, let's go to the schoolroom."

Once she had Justin and Carrie settled, she hurried to Lawrence's room to see what she could do to help. She blamed herself for his illness. She should have paid closer attention when she heard him sniffling the last couple of days. She prayed it hadn't turned into something terrible. He had played quite vigorously in the woods, and it was possible he may have become overheated, what with it being such a warm day.

When she entered Lawrence's room, she heard the poor child whimper. Warren had a basin ready in the event that his son needed to throw up again. Amelia dampened a wash cloth and went over to the bed to help him. After setting the basin down, he accepted the wet cloth and wiped the boy's brow. At least he was awake. She went to the chest of drawers and pulled out a nightshirt and went back to the bed. "Here, let me remove his soiled clothes and put his nightshirt on before the doctor comes."

Warren stepped back to give her room. Amelia quickly changed Lawrence and tucked him into bed. His flushed cheeks and forehead were hot to the touch. She wished the doctor would come, so they could find out what was wrong. Looking over at Warren, she asked, "How long will it be before the doctor gets here?"

"It will take him at least an hour to make it here, unless he's out on another call. Dr. Bentley lives two miles from town in this direction."

Lawrence croaked, "Mama, I'm thirsty."

"I will get you some water, sweetheart." Amelia went over to the dresser and poured water into a glass. When she returned to the bed, she started to hand it to him, but then realized he was too weak to sit. Putting her arm around his shoulders, she raised him so he could drink. "Warren, has your son had chickenpox or scarlet fever, any of the usual childhood illnesses?"

With a frown creasing his brow, he shook his head. "No, he's never been sick before. Lord, I hope he doesn't have one of those diseases. Don't those illnesses usually cause rashes? I don't see anything of that nature on Lawrence."

"I don't see any bumps either. The symptoms are closer to influenza. I did hear him sniffling yesterday. Let us hope it's just a bad cold. That doesn't explain the vomiting, though. That's why I suspect influenza. I suppose we will need to wait for the doctor to know for sure."

Amelia continued bathing his fevered brow while they waited for the doctor. After what seemed like hours, there was a knock on the door and the doctor entered.

After Warren introduced the doctor to her, Dr. Bentley examined Lawrence. "My lord, he has influenza. I have had several cases in town this past week. I will leave you some medicine for the little lordship. I suggest you give him some tepid baths which should keep his temperature from getting any higher. You can feed him gruel and clear soups, but no solid foods. I shall return tomorrow morning to check on him."

He shook the physician's hand. "Thank you, Doctor, for coming. I will do as you suggest. I pray my son shall be improved by morning."

After Dr. Bentley left the room, Amelia rang for a maid. While they waited for her arrival, she pressed a cool cloth to her stepson's forehead. "I'll have the maid prepare a bath for Lawrence. Try not to worry, my lord. I'm sure the medicine will help. I will watch him for you today. I shan't leave his side."

"I can't ask you to do that. I will watch over him."

"I nursed my brother and sister through the chickenpox a few months ago, so I know what he needs." After a light tap on the door, the maid entered, and Amelia gave her instructions for the tepid bath.

"Then I shall leave him in your capable hands. Thank you, my dear. I will gladly accept your assistance. And, I do have a meeting with Monroe. I will come back to check on him after I'm finished. Please let me know if there's any change." After brushing a kiss on his son's forehead, he left the room.

Amelia spent the rest of the day tending Lawrence. His fever climbed higher and higher, and the cough grew much worse. Warren returned, but he paced back and forth to the point that she finally told him to retire, promising to wake him if she needed him. All through the night, she continued to bathe him in tepid water. His fever would go down immediately following the bath, and then soar even higher an hour later.

Warren showed up at dawn and sent Amelia to her room. She only took time to check on Carrie and Justin and change her clothes, before she returned to the sick room. Dr. Bentley returned around nine o'clock to check on Lawrence. There wasn't much he could do, other than offering to bleed him, which Warren flatly refused to allow. She agreed with him, because she remembered when the doctor had bled her stepmother when she had influenza and it hadn't helped her.

Over the next three days, neither Amelia nor Warren left Lawrence's side for more than a few hours at a time. It was heart wrenching to watch Lawrence literally waste away before their eyes. When the tepid baths quit working, Amelia grew desperate as she tirelessly worked to bring his fever down. She had cold water carried from the spring and bathed him with it.

That seemed to help, so she continued giving him the cold water baths four times a day.

When Dr. Bentley came on the fourth day, he looked grave after examining the child. "If this fever doesn't break by tomorrow, I fear your son may not make it. I'm sorry, my lord. He's in God's hands now and only He knows what the outcome will be."

After the doctor left the room, Warren broke down. Tears rolled down his face when he looked at the wasted body of his son. Amelia knelt beside him and gathered him into her arms, and they cried together. "We can't give up, Warren. We must believe he will recover soon. I refuse to accept it. I will not give up hope."

"You heard the doctor," he barked out the words between his tears. "He's given up. I can't lose him. Please…help me."

"I will do whatever is needed. Lawrence *will* recover. Now, you've been up all night with him. I've had a few hours of sleep, so please go to your room and get some rest, at least for a few hours. I promise I will call you if anything changes."

After much persuasion, Amelia convinced him to go lie down. Her heart ached for him. She could tell he felt helpless and was losing hope. While Warren didn't say it, he was obviously devastated at the thought of losing his last link with Lucinda if Lawrence didn't pull through.

All through the day, she labored to bring the child's fever down. It had to break soon, or they would lose him. She turned to prayer since she had done everything else. Falling to her knees, she pleaded, *"Dear Lord, please help me. Give me the strength to nurse Lawrence through this horrid illness. My husband needs his son. I fear he'll lose all reason to live if he loses him. Be with Warren through this ordeal. Let him feel Your comfort. I know I haven't prayed for a long time. I ask that You hear me now. Please let Lawrence live. Amen."*

By the time Amelia finished praying tears cascaded down her face. She dried her eyes on her apron, more determined than ever to pull Lawrence and her husband through this ordeal. With God's help, she *would* prevail.

Chapter 11

Exhausted, Warren fell asleep as soon as his head hit the pillow. When he woke up, he groggily looked over at the clock on the mantle. Oh God, it was after eight o'clock. He jumped out of bed. Fear raced through his thundering heart. Dammit, he had slept for eight hours. Why hadn't Amelia awakened him? Oh, God, please let Lawrence be all right.

Warren dashed to the bathing room. After splashing some water on his face, he hastened to his son's room. Amelia must be exhausted. She had rarely left Lawrence's side for more than a few hours at a time. He didn't know how he would have managed this past week without her. She had taken better care of his son than he would have expected of someone who wasn't his mother, though in Amelia's heart, Lawrence was as precious to her as if she had given birth to him.

The brick wall around his heart cracked, as an overwhelming rush of love filled his soul. He had allowed Amelia to slip under his shield as he watched her tireless determination to keep Lawrence alive. He loved her, loved her fiercely and irrevocably. What amazed him, he felt no guilt. His vision clouded and when it cleared, he saw Lucinda, and she was smiling down at him, nodding her head. Then he heard her voice.

"My love, go to her. Our son will be fine. Her love has saved him — and you. You have the chance to have happiness and joy in your life. There's no reason for you to feel any guilt over loving her. This is what I want for you. Loving her will not lessen what you and I had. I promise your heart is big enough for you to love both of us — each of us in a different way."

"God, Lucinda, I've missed you so much. You're right. I can love both of you. I wish I could touch you, hold you one last time, just to say goodbye."

She floated down to him, smiling into his eyes. She tenderly wrapped her arms around him and while he couldn't feel her touch, he felt an incredible sense of peace and warmth come over him as she whispered, *"Go, my love…go to her and our son…and live a happy life."*

Then she faded away.

Warren stumbled back against the wall. Disoriented, he shook his head to clear it. But the sense of peace stayed with him. Lucinda's unconditional love surrounded him and filled his heart. While he would probably never see or hear from her again, his heart told him she would always be there just beyond sight watching over him and their son and keeping them safe. Her love transcended time and space. All she wanted for them was love and happiness.

The rest of the wall around his heart came tumbling down as he rushed to his son's room. No fear remained because he firmly believed Lawrence would be restored to health. Lucinda told him so.

When he threw open the door, Amelia looked at him, a radiant smile on her face. "Warren. His fever broke a few minutes ago. He just told me he wants something to eat. Isn't that wonderful?"

"Yes, yes it is. It's a miracle." He went to her and wrapped her in his arms. Unabashed tears flowed from his eyes when he looked down at his son. He wrapped Amelia in his arms and tenderly kissed her lips, then murmured, "Thank you. Your determination and will saved him. You never gave up even after the doctor told us it was hopeless. I will be eternally grateful to you for the rest of my life."

Then with the resilience of a child, Lawrence asked, "Papa, after I eat, can I go play with Justin and Carrie?"

He knelt beside his son's bed and hugged him close. "Once the doctor says you are strong enough, you can. Now rest, while we send for some food. I think a nice bowl of porridge is what you need." He turned to Amelia and asked, "Don't you agree, my dear?"

"Yes, it will be perfect for him. I shall order it right now."

After Lawrence ate his porridge, he fell asleep. This time it was a restful, healing sleep. Dr. Bentley came later that morning and pronounced Lawrence well on his way to recovery. Smiling down at the child, he patted his shoulder. "My lord, you should be up and playing in a couple of days. Now, obey your stepmother and eat all your vegetables." Turning toward them, he gave additional reassurance. "He will recover completely. I recommend you keep him quiet for another couple of days. Feed him a bland diet which will help him build his strength. I'm astonished at the difference from yesterday. Albeit, children do tend to recover faster than adults, but even taking that into account, this is a miracle."

After Warren escorted the doctor out, he returned to his son's room. Amelia must be exhausted after staying up with his son with so little sleep. With a kiss on her forehead, he insisted that she go lie down for a few hours. With a weary smile, she caressed his cheek and left the room.

Warren spent the rest of the morning sitting beside his son's bed watching him sleep. He didn't know what to think of the vision he'd had of Lucinda. Although, he had never believed ghosts or spirits existed, he'd been wide awake when he saw and heard her. He had no choice, but to accept that she did indeed appear to him. Her message came through loud and clear. She wanted his happiness and felt Amelia was the answer.

A breath of relief filled him. Deep down in the darkest far reaches of his heart, he had known his feelings for Amelia were different from the first moment he met her hazel-eyed gaze. He had realized she would change his life.

It surprised him that he felt no guilt over loving her, after having at first felt such a sense of betrayal if he had allowed himself to care for her. Lucinda's appearance had released him, giving him the freedom to love again. Lucinda was his first love and always would be. If she had lived, he felt sure their feelings would have deepened into a deep abiding love that would have lasted the rest of their lives, but it wasn't meant to be. Amelia was his soul mate. She fulfilled all his deepest yearnings both physically and emotionally, and she would for the rest of his life.

Looking over at his son, Warren gave thanks that Amelia had come into his life, not only for him, but for Lawrence as well. The love she had for the boy was unconditional, as a mother's love needed to be. He wanted her love too. They were definitely compatible sexually, but he wanted so much more from her than that.

His heart ached when he remembered how harsh he had been with her the last time they were intimate. He now realized his reaction was because she had wormed her way into his heart, and he felt threatened. There had been such a great deal of hurt in her eyes when he had lashed out at her on several occasions. He had a great many amends he needed to make. What seemed to hurt her most — his lack of trust. While it would be difficult, he would not only have to bare his soul to her, he would have to let her see his scars. That scared the hell out of him, because if she turned away in disgust it would tear his heart from his chest.

He would go to her tonight and let her see his scars before he told her he loved her. That way if she turned away from him he could at least hold onto some of his pride. There was no way he would tell her of his change of heart if she couldn't bear to look at him.

What he *would* do, no matter how difficult, he would take a look at himself in the mirror. Amelia had told him the scars might not be as bad as he remembered. After all, it was three years since he had looked at them. With that settled, he relaxed against the back of the chair. Lawrence had awakened, so he turned his focus back on him. "Good afternoon, young man. I imagine you're hungry. I will ring for some lunch."

Lawrence pushed himself to a sitting position. "I'm starving. May I have some pudding if I eat all my food? When may I see Justin and Carrie?"

"Later this afternoon. After you eat your lunch, I want you to take another nap. Then if you feel up to it when you awaken, I'll allow you to see them for a brief visit. Remember what the doctor told you. He wants you to stay in bed for the next two days so you can gain your strength back."

"I already feel much better, but *all* right, I shall do as you ask." Then with a shudder, he added, "I hope I'm never ill again. It felt horrible."

Hearing a knock on the door, he called out, "Come in." Katie, the nursemaid, entered with a lunch tray. After Lawrence ate, including the vanilla custard Mrs. Jarvis sent up for him, Warren tucked him in and he fell fast asleep. The nursemaid agreed to sit with his son while he slept, and he left, knowing Lawrence was on the road to recovery.

Warren went to Amelia's room, and found her sleeping. While he watched her slumber, a fierce need came over him. He longed to lie beside her and hold her close, to stroke her lovely skin and show her how he felt. Although his need was fierce, he would refrain because she needed her rest. Tonight would be a different story. Then he would do more than hold her. Tonight he would make love to her. He realized they had never made love. Oh, they'd had sex many times, but love hadn't had anything to do with it.

No tonight, he would open himself up to her in a way he had never done before with any woman since Lucinda. A surge of energy rushed through him when he thought of the night to come, but then shards of icy fear raced through him. What if she turned away from him in disgust?

Oh, God, I will be crushed.

No, he refused to let fear rule his life anymore. Tonight, he would put all that behind him. He had to believe she returned *some* of his feelings. He had caught her looking at him with longing several times. He remembered how giving she had been last week, when she made love to his cock. She wouldn't have done that if she didn't have strong feelings for him. He knew enough about women to know that when it came to sucking a man's cock, normally only prostitutes did that. Amelia had acted as if she enjoyed it as much as he had. Her eyes had glowed with arousal, and she had told him she wanted to give him pleasure. Bending down, he brushed a feather light kiss on her brow so he wouldn't wake her. Then he silently left her room.

After he went to his bedchamber, he went down to his study, where he spent the afternoon with Monroe going over reports and catching up on estate business he had neglected while Lawrence was ill. Thoughts of what he would do that night bothered his concentration, but he pushed them from his mind for the most part. At six o'clock, he called it a day and went upstairs to dress for dinner.

Once he visited Lawrence to make sure he was still recovering, he went to his rooms and dressed for the evening. Nervous anticipation rushed through him as he made his way down to the drawing room. When he entered, Amelia sat on the sofa looking well-rested and relaxed.

Meeting his gaze, she gave him a welcoming smile. "Did you get any work done this afternoon? Your valet told me you were in your study with Monroe."

"Yes, but it will take several days to catch up. I checked on Lawrence before I dressed for dinner. He's definitely feeling much better. It's amazing how fast he's recovering."

"When I woke up, I checked on him as well. I agree. He's certainly bouncing back quickly. I allowed Justin and Carrie to see him and read them a story. He's already feeling the constraints of the sick bed. We're going to have a hard time keeping him quiet tomorrow." As she finished speaking, Abercrombie came in and announced dinner.

Warren offered Amelia his arm. "Come, my dear, shall we go in to dinner? Then patting her hand, he added, "I'm glad you slept most of the day. You deserve it after the past week."

"I'll admit it. I was quite exhausted, but I'm feeling fine now."

After Warren helped her take her seat, he took his. "I can tell. You look ravishing tonight." Keeping the conversation light, they discussed some of the workings of the estate. After dinner, they went to the library and read for a while. At ten o'clock, he smiled over at her. "I'm ready to retire. I would like to join you."

Fire glowed in the depths of her hazel eyes, turning them to green. She gave him a coy smile. "I would love to have you come to me tonight."

Her look sent tendrils of pleasure racing straight to his loins, but not wanting to appear too eager, he smoothly offered, "Let me walk you to your room, and I will join you in thirty minutes."

After leaving Amelia at her door, he quickly entered his room. Hendricks had laid out a dressing gown and night shirt on the end of the bed and left for the night. Nervous over what he was about to do, he took a quick wash and a shave, and then poured a glass of brandy to calm his nerves.

Lord, please don't let her be repulsed by my scars.

With the time of truth upon him, he moved over to the mirror, but kept his back to it. Taking off his shirt, he slowly turned around and opened his eyes. Afraid to believe what he saw, he stepped closer. The scars were no longer red and angry. While they were still visible, they had faded considerably. While he didn't have any hair on his chest anymore, he didn't look grotesque. He ran a bare hand over the scarred flesh. Now that he had seen the scars, the feel of them wasn't as horrid.

If he blew out most of the candles, and just left the wall sconces burning, she might not be repulsed. Hope blossomed inside him. He reached for the nightshirt, but then he let it fall to the floor. He would leave it off and wear the dressing gown alone. Once he had it on, he took a last look at his reflection. With the robe tied snugly at his waist, the dressing gown only showed a small amount of his chest and hid most of the scars. Girding his loins, he walked to the door, entered his dressing room and swiftly crossed it to the door leading to Amelia's room. Taking a deep breath, he closed a shaking hand around the door knob. Turning it, he pushed open the door.

Amelia stood by the window with her glorious auburn tresses flowing down her back. Walking up behind her, he pulled her back against him. "I love your soft hair." The scent of jasmine and lavender wafted up as he pushed her curls to the side, intoxicating him. He turned her around and pulled her close, then gave her a tender kiss. He picked her up and carried her to the bed, gently lying her down. "I'll put out some of this light."

Warren went around the room, blowing out all the candles, except the wall sconces. He turned down the lamp on the bedside table to a soft glow. Ever so slowly, he untied the sash, letting the dressing gown fall open. He closed his eyes, afraid of what he would see in her gaze. He allowed the robe to fall to the floor. He heard a rustling of the bed clothes, and then he felt

Amelia's gentle touch. He slowly opened his eyes, and she smiled up at him.

She leaned forward and placed a kiss in the middle of his chest. "See I told you they wouldn't be bad. I can hardly see them at all," she whispered as she rained kisses all over his chest.

He had to blink several times to keep tears from falling. Amelia wasn't repulsed by the scars. She caressed his chest with her lips. A wealth of love overflowed his being. Gently lifting her chin, he reverently kissed her lips, stroking the edge, licking the surface, unable to get enough of her sweet taste. Amelia moaned as she parted her lips, allowing his tongue to invade the recess of her mouth. Soon their tongues were dueling, each of them unable to get close enough to the other. He gently pushed her down to the silken sheets and followed her, wrapping his arms around her, cocooning her in his embrace.

Kissing every surface of her face, he murmured, "My beautiful wife." He gently ran the back of his hand down her cheek. "Let me show you how much I care," nibbling his way down her neck, then her chest, on to her breast, licking and stroking her delicate skin as he continued to whisper sweet words of love.

His heart exploded as he took her turgid nipple into his mouth, gently sucking and licking her areola, drawing circles around it. Fierce flames raced through him and down to his prick, sending fire to his balls. Continuing on his path, he licked and stroked his way to her navel, swirling his tongue around it, then down her belly until he reached the apex of her thighs. The scent of her arousal filled his senses, making him slightly light-headed.

As he stroked her tight bud, she gasped and moved her hips, getting as close as possible to his exploring tongue. While licking the hooded nubbin, he slid his middle finger into her warm channel. Her crème came gushing out, soaking his fingers. Her passage clinched around his finger as he slid another one in. By this time, Amelia's breathing was shallow. She took short little panting breaths with each stroke of his fingers. Sensing she was close, he sucked deeply on her clitoris and felt her come apart, as he lapped up her delicious crème, sweet, yet tangy at the same time. He continued lightly stroking and licking around her point of desire, prolonging her climax, drawing it out of her, hearing her high keening cry.

Rising up, he kissed her lips as he positioned himself at the entrance of her sheath. With one thrust, he was in, feeling sensation upon sensation all the way to his nerve endings. Slowly, oh so slowly, he pulled back, just leaving the tip of his shaft inside, then he slid back in to the hilt. He moaned. The veins in his cock pulsed when he repeated his powerful thrusts again and again. Unable to continue his slow thrusts, he picked up the pace, stroking in and out, faster and harder.

Amelia's head thrashed back and forth on the pillow, and her cries filled the air. Satisfied that she had found her release, Warren let himself go, stroking faster and faster. Just when he thought he would expire from the pleasure of it all, his seed burst forth, filling her with his essence, his heart pounding from the sheer magnitude of the climax. His arms gave way and he slumped against her breasts. Knowing his weight was too much for her, he rolled to the side, pulling her with him and cradled her close.

She dropped her head back down on his chest with a contented sigh. He stroked her smooth shoulders. "My love, you're the mate of my soul. I love you, Amelia. When I join my body to yours, we truly become one."

Looking up, she gave him a sated smile. "Oh, my love, I feel the same way. You're my missing piece and now I feel whole. I love you more than life itself. I've realized it from the start."

Pulling her up, he kissed her with all the love and tenderness he had in his heart. At last, he was ready…to live again. Then he showed her all over again—how much he loved her to the depths of his soul.

Epilogue

Within a few days, Lawrence was up and playing as if he had never been ill. Amelia loved spending her days with the children and her nights with her husband, reaching heights of passion she never dreamed possible. Her love for him knew no bounds, and he told her he felt the same way.

Warren needed to return to London, since there was another big vote coming up in Parliament, but he refused to leave her or the children behind. The following Monday, they loaded the carriages and made the trip back to town.

Life settled into a pattern once they returned to London. Warren spent some mornings with Humphries, and others with Lord Rutherford. Three afternoons a week were spent at the House of Lords. Amelia spent mornings making social calls with Sophie, and afternoons, playing in the park with the children. On Wednesday night, they attended Almack's, then

Saturday, either a ball, the opera or a play. Amelia found out she adored the theater.

The days turned to weeks, and no matter how busy her husband was or how late they stayed out, he still found the energy to make deep satisfying love to her. Since they had shared their feelings for each other, lovemaking reached new heights of blistering passion.

At the end of the Parliament session, they returned to Broadmoor Manor. When the carriage entered the drive, a rush of joy filled Amelia's heart and tears moistened her eyes, home at last. While she had enjoyed spending time with Sophie, she had grown quite tired from all the nightly entertainments. The peace of home rejuvenated her spirit.

The end of the summer passed with long lazy days spent with the children, and passion-filled nights spent in her loving husband's embrace. Many afternoons were spent at the lake teaching all three children how to fish. Justin and Carrie learned to ride and Warren bought ponies for both. As a family, they raced through the open fields and explored the many wooded paths on the estate.

Fall came and Warren had another exceptional harvest. He held a festival for all of his tenants and workers. Amelia actively participated in planning all the games and contests. They ended the day with a huge bonfire, where they danced long into the night. It was one of the most enjoyable nights of her life.

When they returned to the house, they carried the children to bed and made their way to their rooms. As Warren left her at her door, he told her, "I'll join you in fifteen minutes, my love." Then he kissed her cheek and went down the hall to his bedchamber.

Amelia watched as he went through the door to his room, admiring his well-muscled backside. Chills ran up and down her spine, even though they made love most nights, each time felt as the first had. After, she entered her room, she hurried through her nightly ritual. All aquiver from the exciting news she planned to share with her husband, she wanted to make the night special. She donned her new emerald green, silk night rail, which was so transparent it revealed her more generous curves. Over the last six months she had added some weight. Once she finished her ablutions, she climbed into her bed to await Warren.

With a light tap on the door, he entered. "Ah, now that's a magnificent sight. I love it when you let down your glorious hair." Since the need to keep himself covered no longer existed, he untied his dark blue banyan and laid it across the foot of the bed. Her mouth went dry as she drank in the sight of Warren in full arousal. His large erection stood at attention and sent a delicious swirl of flames to her drenched core. Her eyes drank in his broad shoulders and well-defined chest.

Amelia gave him a come hither smile. "Come here, husband. Let me feast on your cock."

Warren approached the bed, and she reached over and stroked his heavily engorged prick. Slipping from the bed, she took him into the deep cavern of her mouth and greedily sucked. One hand crept up and played with his flat male nipples while the other hand stroked his balls as her lips lavished attention on his thick shaft. Glancing up, she watched as his eyes closed from the sheer pleasure he must be feeling. It gave her immense satisfaction, knowing she had him in her thrall.

Warren moaned and reached down, pulling her up into his arms as he gave her a bruising kiss. "While I enjoy having your delectable lips wrapped around my cock, I want to be inside you tonight." He tumbled her down to the bed, spread her legs wide and slid home. "Damn, I love your wet pussy."

Stroking deep, he set a vigorous pace, pounding into her over and over again. Her passions ignited as a vortex of searing heat rushed through her entire body. The tension continued building while Warren stroked faster and deeper into her burning hot portal. Reveling in the ability to touch and stroke her husband's body when that had been denied in the beginning, Amelia wrapped her legs around his slim hips, pulling him closer as she toyed with his nipples, something she'd found that seemed to bring Warren immense pleasure. His heady scent of clean masculine sweat wafted around her, sending her passion even higher.

He reached down between their bodies and squeezed her clitoris, sending her spiraling off into the abyss. Her passage milked his cock as his seed filled her to the brim. Amelia let out a scream when he buried himself one last time inside her, sending them both spinning off into oblivion. Warren groaned as he withdrew and rolled to the side, then pulled her close. Giving her a tender kiss on her temple, they lay in blissful peace as their hearts slowed down and their breathing evened out. "I'll never have enough of you, my dearest heart...I love you, Amelia."

"I love you too, Warren." Sighing, she cuddled close and placed her hand over his heart. "I visited Dr. Bentley yesterday."

He lifted her chin and looked gravely into her eyes. "My love, are you ill?" Alarm radiated in his voice.

Giving him a tremulous smile, she shook her head. "No, not ill, but I hope you don't mind, I shall get fat over the next seven months. The doctor confirmed what I had suspected…I'm with child, my love."

"Oh, my heart, you've made me the happiest of men. I never dreamed I would find such joy as you have brought me, and now a babe. I'm greatly pleased, my darling. Your love consumes my soul, beyond anything I could have ever imagined." He gave her a kiss filled with wonder and awe, then with a smile on his face, he closed his eyes.

Amelia sighed as intense emotions swirled through her being, thanking God for bringing Warren to her that scary spring night. Things could have turned out so differently, if she hadn't met him. Not only had God given her the love of an honorable man, he gave her Lawrence, the child of her heart and now the anticipation of a new babe in the spring to look forward to. Life was good. She had just settled against her beloved's chest when something caught her eye.

A shadow formed by the window. Amelia couldn't quite make out what it was. Curiosity getting the best of her, she slipped from the bed and pulled on her dressing gown. She moved toward the area and a beautiful woman with flowing auburn hair appeared. The woman spoke to her. "*I give you my son and my dearest love. I knew you were what they needed. Keep them safe and love them well.*"

Amelia whispered, "Thank you for sending them to me. I promise, I shall love and protect both of them forever."

The ghost, who could only be Warren's late wife, smiled. Then with a wave of her hand, she faded away. While Amelia had never believed in spirits, no fear filled her heart, only joy and thankfulness. She went back to the bed and stood there listening to Warren's deep, slow breathing. She felt at peace with her world. She had received a most precious gift—Lucinda's blessing.

The End

About the Author

Vikki Vaught, writing as V.L. Edwards, started her writing career when a story invaded her mind and would not leave. Over the last few years, she has written more than a half dozen historical romances and is presently working on her next. *To Live Again* is her debut novel in erotic historical romance. She also has another recent release, writing as Vikki Vaught. *Lady Overton's Perilous Journey* is the first book in her Honorable Rogue series.

Vikki loves a "Happily Ever After," and she writes them in her stories. While romance is the central theme of all her books, she includes some significant historical event or place in all her novels.

While all her books are love stories, she has also written sweet contemporary romances as Vikki McCombie.

Vikki lives in the beautiful foothills of the Smoky Mountains of Tennessee with her beloved husband, Jim, who is the most tolerant man in the world to put up with her when she is in a writing frenzy. When she isn't writing or working her day job, you'll find her curled up in a comfortable chair reading her Kindle, lost in a good book with a cup of tea at her side..

Website: http://www.vikkivaught.com/home.html
Email: vvaught512@aol.com
Facebook: https://www.facebook.com/VikkiVaught
Twitter: https://twitter.com/vvaught512
Google+: https://plus.google.com/u/0/+VikkiMcCombie/posts
Pinterest: https://www.pinterest.com/vaughtmccombie/
Amazon Author Page: http://smile.amazon.com/Vikki-Vaught/e/B008EE7TG2/ref=sr_tc_2_0?qid=1433778387&sr=1-2-ent
Goodreads Author Page: https://www.goodreads.com/author/show/5208041.Vikki_Vaught